THE
DEADLY WINTER

By
Arthur H. Norby

Copyright © 2014
Revised 2019 and 2022

Arthur H. Norby

* * * * *

Cover photo by Kari L. Barchenger

Disclaimer
This is a work of fiction, a product of the author's imagination. Any resemblance or similarity to any actual events or persons, living or dead, is purely coincidental. Although the author and publisher have made every effort to ensure there are no errors, inaccuracies, omissions, or inconsistencies herein, any slights or people, places, or organizations are unintentional.

ACKNOWLEDGEMENTS

I would like to acknowledge the endless hours put in by my wife Kathryn Spangler Norby for transcribing my early notes, dealing with the computer and graphics. My thanks also go to my daughter Kari Barchenger for photography and cover design, my daughter Kelly Pickle for proof reading and editing, and Kelly's husband Craig for being the model on the cover.

Finally, to my father Harlan P. Norby, I give a special thanks for the stories of his youth and told to me over the years, without which this tale could not be told.

Set in rural Minnesota in 1938, the death of a transient worker on a Works Project Administration construction project, known universally as "the WPA," is just the beginning of a series of deaths culminating in one last event bringing justice to the community. This is a historically based narrative without a specific hero. It is a story describing the prejudices affecting an entire community, from laborers and farmers to merchants and Native Americans, to lovers and law enforcement.

FOREWARD

As a young man growing up in the farm country of Minnesota, I took for granted the stories of the good old days—as we usually think of our own history—and I gave no thought to past murders. I listened raptly to the tales told by my father, uncles, and grandfather, and my life has been enriched by the simple stories and descriptions of people I would never meet.

Although raised in the county seat of Montevideo, my roots were in the farmlands of Chippewa, Swift, and Lac Qui Parle counties. My ancestors were among the early settlers in that area near the headwater of the Minnesota River. The Norbys, Cantons, Overlands, Iversons, and Seversons came singly or as entire families, from Norway, usually through the Great Lakes, then on across Wisconsin and Iowa, to homestead the hilly farm country of Minnesota that had just become a state in 1858. They married and raised their families and grew old, a part of the land. Some moved again to homestead still more distant land, while some returned to their native Norway. And for generations these farm people have told their stories to their children and to the newcomers of their community.

Among the stories I had heard many times was that of a stranger, a transient laborer who worked on the flood control project, whose body was discovered, run over during a winter storm by one of the local residents. A violent and callous act showing no regard for the sanctity of life, the truth of this tale was reinforced each time it was told, the facts more reliable.

During the 1930's the farm communities of Minnesota, along with farmers across the country, suffered the effects of persistent drought. Unlike many of the plains states however, parts of Minnesota—drought or no—were still flooded annually when the spring snow and ice melts surged into the river valleys. Since the end of the last ice age these floods had been an annual threat, but by the twentieth century they also became recognized as a financial hazard, and in 1936 a major flood control project, by the United States government, was undertaken in order to alleviate or at least minimize the flooding along the course of the Minnesota River.

The Corps of Army Engineers, through the Works Projects Administration, began to build a series of flood control dams which would alter river flooding all the way to the Gulf of Mexico. Men like the transient Ernie Hall came from all over the country. Some came by accident of circumstance, while others arrived intentionally with purpose, motive, and desires. Still suffering from the drought and depression that plagued the country, they became part of one of the largest WPA projects in the land.

As I grew older and had heard the story of the killing of the transient worker many times, I recognized for the first time a strong flavor of prejudice from my father as he related this tale. Those prejudices were not his alone, but an accumulation of attitudes which were woven into the fabric of the community and affected that entire generation. I began to hear the stories from my father's youth with an entirely new understanding. A new doorway to my own life began to slowly open before me.

In his telling of the story, I was surprised at my father's disdain for this transient. To my thinking Ernie Hall was just a man struggling to stay employed in post-depression Minnesota. He was a man whom I now saw from a future perspective to be in the same circumstances as many others struggling on farms or railroads, or wherever it was possible to eke out a living during those hard times. But my father showed an entirely different attitude toward him.

I recognized, however, that my father's prejudice was not an intentional attitude, but a subconscious animosity developed over the half-century of his life, of remembering people who had lived in his community, people who came from other places, and when their needs had been met, moved once more out of his life. Nor was this prejudice unique to my father or even to this group of people. I thought then that perhaps we are all victims of our unrecognized prejudice, living with the results of histories we don't always understand, not taking time to understand.

The location of the Lac Qui Parle River dam, the surrounding communities and roads connecting them exist today The farms, businesses and people in this story however are purely fictional, as are so many of our memories.

Chapter One

March 9, 1938

"There's no such thing as a quiet murder, is there, Ernie?" Tom Hall slouched on the depot's hard wooden bench as he spoke to his brother. Ernie did not reply. Ernie was in the large casket next to Tom, awaiting his final train-ride home. The rain continued in an unseasonal torrent and was driven across the streets and across the depot platform by a bitter March wind.

Tom knew that before long the rain would turn to a heavy wet snow. He would be far more content when he was watching the weather from the lounge car as the train took him back to Ohio. For now he could only endure the rain in the hollow silence of the depot. As the rain pummeled the building around him its hypnotic rhythm drew his thoughts back to Ohio, and to the beginning of his strange odyssey.

It had been an ordinary February afternoon when Tom stepped off the train in Marion, Ohio, hoping to finally spend some real family time with his mother. Although he was stationed in Washington, D.C. his assignment as an attaché had taken him out of the country frequently. Most of his duties were very ordinary, but none the less he was seldom able to get to Ohio.

Before the Navy he attended Ohio State, and went home on occasional breaks, but he had worked summers right at the college and didn't get to see Mom or his brother Ernie often. As a matter of fact, he recalled he hadn't seen his brother since leaving for officer candidate school. After receiving his commission he'd received orders to Washington DC and had spent only a few days since then with his mother. Ernie had been working out west Mom said, and Tom hadn't seen his older brother during the few trips back home.

Now it felt great to be coming home again. As he followed the familiar tree lined street toward his parents' cottage Tom remembered the glorious days growing up here; the days before the depression, before the mills and plants closed, before he had left Marion. Tom was eager to see Ernie.

Ernie had been just like a father to Tom. In fact he was the only father Tom could remember. Tom had been a baby when his dad died, and the burden of providing for the family fell on Ernie. Not only did Ernie see that Tom was raised properly, but he also made sure Tom got a good education. There was never any question about Tom's future as far as Ernie was concerned. Tom was going to college. There would be no arguments. Thanks to Ernie he had finished college and had received his Navy commission.

Ernie hadn't the good fortune, or perhaps he just hadn't had the aptitude to go to college. There was a time Tom felt guilty about receiving his education while Ernie had been hard at work providing for him and Mom, but he knew now that every young man wasn't cut out for hard academic study.

It had been great growing up with Ernie, an older brother who had always been there when Tom needed him. "I'm almost old enough to be your old man," Ernie had said many times. "You were an accident for the folks. I remember I was just finishing high school when all of a sudden Mom found herself pregnant. She thought I didn't know how upset she was, but I heard her and Dad talking about it, wondering how they could afford another baby, how she was going to be able to just have a baby at her age. By then she was almost forty years old and she was worried. Having another baby was the last thing she wanted."

"Once you were born, however, there were no regrets. You were a good kid to have around. I think when Dad died she blessed the Virgin Mary and everyone else for having you. As a matter of fact, I was always glad to have you around. It's too bad Dad didn't live to see you grow up. I know he'd have been as proud as I am."

"I wonder how he's made out with the plants closed," Tom thought now as he neared home. A moment of guilt disturbed Tom as he realized he had never written Ernie a single letter; "tomorrow night, I'm just too tired right now," was always his excuse, but now, "well, I'll see him soon."

The moment he entered his parents' cottage Tom sensed something was wrong. The house was cool and dark, not at all as it had been when he was growing up, not at all as it should have been right now. This was a home that was always happy and cheerful, a home kept lighted by happiness, by the close-knit relationship of a mother and two sons who all loved life and who loved each other. Now the thin cold silence was too quiet and brought a sense of foreboding. As Tom walked through the house he feared something had happened to his mother, but as he neared the living room he could hear his mother crying.

He dropped his travel bag in the hall and in a moment was kneeling at her side. As he looked at his mother her teary eyes blinked up at him. "Oh, Thomas, Thomas," she cried as she saw him. "Ernie's dead."

Tom felt as if he had been hit in the stomach with a sledgehammer. For a moment, his brain convinced him he had misunderstood, but as he watched his mother crying, the realization of truth caught him. His head swam and he felt dizzy at the shock of the news, like he did on that birthday so long ago when, playing pin the tail on the donkey. Ernie had spun him around too many times and he got so dizzy he thought he'd throw up.

Slowly Tom gained control of his senses, as he always did, and faced the awful truth borne to him by his mother. "I'll write tomorrow night…Oh, God! Why didn't I at least write," he anguished. Tom picked up the telegram lying on the table at his mother's side.

"February 2, 1938. Montevideo, Minnesota," it began. *"Dear Mrs. Hall, I'm so sorry to inform you that your son Ernest was recently killed here, in an automobile accident. We have a hit and run driver in custody. Please make arrangements to claim your son's body." Signed sincerely, Carl Brown, Chippewa County Sheriff, Montevideo, Minnesota.*

Tom sat in the chair beside his mother and took her hand. "I'll take care of this, Mom," was all he could think to say. For a long while they sat together in the dark room thinking their own thoughts about Ernie; son, brother, gone from their lives forever.

Now, just three weeks later as he sat in the drafty Minnesota railroad depot, Tom absently reached into his pocket for his pipe. He filled it slowly and with a plain gold lighter held to the bowl he drew deeply several times to bring life into the bed of tobacco. He had crossed half the country since that day and found much more than the cold body of his brother. Now he waited once more for the train to take him home, and as he waited he absently gazed at the string of smoke rings filling the air in front of him and recalled his strange journey to this small Minnesota town.

CHAPTER
TWO

February 16, 1938

For two weeks a formidable weather system had been building, creeping slowly across the Canadian prairie. Each day and each night its progress held spring at bay, demanding still another bone chilling engagement with the land before surrendering to the sun's life-giving spring warmth. The sky had turned a steely gray and the overcast sky modulated the dropping temperature until day and night it now hovered steadily around zero. The clashing of the high and low weather front kicked up gusting winds which amplified the cold temperatures, driving the ice deeper into the earth's unprotected flesh. For a thousand miles the wind had found no resistance from mountains or any other opposing forces but continued drifting over the lakes and forests and the winter-barren prairies. Now, on this late afternoon, the cold was creeping through the hills which surrounded the Minnesota River valley, sending its residents to seek warm shelter.

Although he was unaware of the events to come, Tom Hall felt the tension mount within him as his long train ride to Minnesota was nearing its end and the task of bringing Ernie home began. The river ice crackled in the frigid air and the twin steel ribbons of track rattled as the afternoon Milwaukee Road passenger train had wound its way northwesterly through the valley, cutting across the gusting wind as it powered on towards Montevideo. In a few minutes, the train would stop to release its passengers onto the cold station platform. The train crew would be exchanging the passengers and their baggage along with canvas sacks of mail and other freight for whatever similar cargo might be waiting, rushing to and fro, as if exchanging hostages in the frigid night before plummeting again into the darkness.

Although some of the passengers felt the frigid weather was following them as they headed for their western destinations, the truth was that the storm preceded them and was waiting to welcome each traveler as they left the train's protective warmth, waiting to wrap a sinister winter jacket around a father or a child who might step unprepared from the train, and then wrestle him into the snow where the painful cold would chill him to the bone. Then just for a moment grant a reprieve by turning the pain into drowsiness then warm peaceful, permanent sleep.

Tom pulled his coat close as he stepped from the train and tightened his muffled hat onto his head. Although it was only four p.m. darkness was settling firmly on the little Minnesota community. The pale yellow sun which had fought in vain to break through the gray sky had finally given up its fight and retired over the horizon to gather its strength to fight another day. As he walked to the end of the depot platform Tom flexed the travel stiffness from his body, twisting and bending like a heavily robed fighter entering the arena. It felt good to be free from the train's confines, even to stand here in the frigid darkness.

For a moment Tom stood at the platform's edge and surveyed what was visible of the small town. Streetlights dotted their pale way into the night, following the town's gently sloping main street, which was buried under a blanket of snow, and disappeared frequently when the wind kicked up the fine snow particles, carrying them away into the darkness. The chilly white blanket covered the sidewalks, streets, and naked winter trees equally, showing no compassion as the wind whipped the snow's fine particles to in a frenzy. Only a few tracks showed through the snow where some hardy resident passed on the way to shelter.

Tom turned now to enter the depot, to retrieve his baggage and then continue into the night. A shiver coursed through his body. He would prefer his mission here was over and he was instead entering the warmth of the club car, going home to Ohio. That was still to come. For now he had to endure.

As he turned to enter the station clouds of steam surged from the escape valves under the train. Under the steam and black coal smoke the bronze bell atop the engine anxiously signaled for movement while the conductor waved his lamp to signal his readiness to leave. Then, slowly at first, the engine puffed, filling the air with acrid smoke as the train lurched out of the station and into the night.

No one met Tom at the depot, nor had he expected to be met. The long trip from Ohio had been made in solitude and now he was ready as possible to deal with locating his brother Ernie, bringing him home. Tom rang the service bell on the depot counter. While waiting for the stationmaster he stood looking out once more on the silent inhospitable town.

Through the frost covered windows Tom could see the long sweep of a hilly street which began near at the depot door and stretched beyond his view into the darkness. Perhaps, in the summer it was picturesque, but this afternoon, the town was wrapped in cold wind-driven gusts of snow and the barren street threw up a forbidding barrier. Tom watched as dim headlights crossed on the dark side street before him, followed by a slow moving panel truck. On its side bold black letters announced the passing of a deliveryman from Zaiser's Dairy as he made his way at the end of the day to the dairy's parking garage and then to the warmth of his own home.

"If you've got your stubs, I'll get your bags out for you, young fellow." The depot master, puffed up with the importance and excitement of handling all the arriving and departing activities thrust his hand to Tom, who responded, casually relinquishing the required stub for his one suitcase.

As he collected his bag Tom asked the station master directions to the sheriff's office. "I've a little business with the sheriff. Can you tell me how to get to the courthouse or the jail from here?" He involuntarily shivered at the thought of facing the weather.

"Hah! I can sure tell you that, all right. We've got our courthouse and jail together, right up on Fourth Street and Meridian. I suppose some folks would tell you it's on Third since it takes the whole end of the block, but it's surely on Fourth all right." The station master looked Tom over carefully, smugly assessing the young man who stood ramrod straight in his big-city camel hair coat and snap brim hat. "A dude for sure," he thought.

"You've got a long haul though, lad. That street you see just outside the window there, it leads right to the courthouse. In the summer it's a nice walk, but on a day like today you'll likely freeze your ass off. It's about eight blocks straight up that hill. The courthouse is a big orange brick building just past the First Baptist Church; you can't miss it."

"I don't suppose there's a taxi in town?" Tom knew he was hoping for the impossible.

"We're a little too far from the big city for that, Mister," the man responded. "Out here in the country folks still don't mind walking, you see. Of course you probably won't find anybody around up there today anyhow, being it's after four o'clock. Reckon you might just have a cold walk for nothing."

The thought had occurred to Tom. "If you don't mind, I'll leave that bag here for the time being. After I've seen the sheriff I'll stop back."

"You've heard about our excitement here, though, have you?" The station master had a gleam in his eye. His leer was meant to indicate that perhaps he could tell a story this stranger would like to hear. From his slick looks this guy could just be a reporter from some big newspaper, maybe the Minneapolis Star Tribune or even the St, Paul Pioneer Press. There it would be, "stationmaster quoted as saying…." he could see his name in print even now.

"No," Tom replied. "As a matter of fact, I didn't know your town existed until about a week ago. I've just come from back east to take care of some business. I don't know much about this country except that it's mighty damn cold!" He watched now as the station master's face grew dark and somber as he leaned across the counter and began his gossip. The sparkle in his eye made a lie of his long dour face.

"Well, you see," he pulled his wire legged stool closer to the counter, "we've got this young feller in jail up there. He killed a couple of guys. Yes sir, we've had some excitement here all right, more than I can ever remember around here."

"Warren Marshall is the fellow's name, one of those damn farm kids." Tom couldn't help but notice that the station master seemed irritated or angry just at the mention of "farm kid" as though being a farmer was worse than the fact that he was a murderer.

"Well, he moved to Montevideo about a year or so ago, got a job driving truck for Swift's, one of those big outfits out of St. Paul. They got a plant on the west edge of town, just built a new plant up the street here a ways too. A big operation! Well, his feller just come in and took one of the jobs hauling milk and eggs from creameries around the county, a job one of our boys from town here could have used, I might add. I don't know why Swift's wants to hire them farmers when there're so many of our boys from town still out of work."

"Well, this Marshall, pretty soon he started seeing one of them little farm girls from up by Watson, that's where he's from, too, and then he's been seen carousing all over the county. I seen him around here and there myself. I don't know that he was ever in any real trouble before he moved to town, to tell the truth, but everybody knows how wild he is. Seems to me if the farmers ever expect to make a go of it they can't be running around owl-hooting till all hours. It's no wonder prices on farm goods has gone up so much. Yeah, seems like most of the problems around here these days are brought on by the farmers. Well, it'll catch up with them one of these days."

"Then back in January," the station master continued, "the twenty-ninth, I think it was, we had a big snowstorm here."

"You mean this isn't a storm?" Tom spoke. "I don't think I've ever felt this cold in my life!"

"Oh, this is nothing. Some folks seem to think it was awfully late for a big storm, it being the end of January, but lots of years before the drought we got big storms way out into March, even remember on year we got a bad storm the first part of April. Well, it snowed and blew for three days. Started on a Saturday, when all this happened. Before it was over, I guess every road in the county was blocked shut by the snow. In some places, there was drifts five, six feet high, or maybe higher. When Doc Burns was called out to Ole Barsness's to fix his kid's broken leg, Doc had to take his horse and cutter, couldn't even get out of town with a car."

Although Tom was beginning to feel agitated by the station master's digressing, he hitched his patience together and waited for the point of the story to be made. Perhaps it was the thought of the cold walk that kept Tom's patience in check.

"In spite of the storm, which kept most of the sane people home, young Marshall and his girlfriend spent the night drinking and dancing, so I'm told, out at Buster's, a little

beer joint west of Watson. Then, with a snootful of liquor they headed out into the storm. That's when he ran over this fellow and killed him. Of course that fellow was just one of the transients working on the new dam out there, not like it was one of our locals, you know"

"The government is building a new dam, you see, on the Minnesota River up by Watson. Well, hard as work is to find these days, we get lots of fellows from all over the country showing up to work out there. With all the dikes and dams they're building out there along the river bottom I guess there's twenty-five hundred men working around there. They even built a big camp for the transients right there by the dam. Seems to me, some of them transients live better than we do in town. They sure create havoc, too. Then, on paydays, they're all over the county drinking and chasing our women. No, I guess we won't miss one or two of them."

"I suppose the guy was walking into Watson for some of that cheap booze that night when this drunken farm kid—him and his girlfriend—ran over him. They left him in a snowbank and just kept on going their merry way."

In Tom's mind the image of the accident was clear. It might have been the wind creeping into the depot sparked his imagination, but he could visualize the storm, the unsuspecting Ernie trudging through the night, then in an instant the lights of the speeding car overtook him. Before Ernie could jump aside, the driver slammed into him, and in a drunken stupor fled into the night, hoping to escape in the storm and never be connected to the man's death. As Tom opened his mouth to respond the depot attendant continued his tale.

"That wasn't the end, of course. As luck would have it the sheriff came along just a few minutes after it happened. It took all night, but finally he tracked young Marshall down and arrested him, threw him in jail all right. They charged Marshall with manslaughter. Then, a couple of days later, they let him out on bail while they got everything ready to go to trial."

"Well, while he was out of jail, this Marshall got into a big brouhaha with Timmy Coyle, one of the kids from town. I don't suppose Timmy was really a kid any more though, must have been twenty-five or twenty-six years old by now. He was a good kid, from a real good family, too. Me and his old man have been friends for years."

The fact was the Coyle family had little time for the station master or his gossip. The professional courtesy shown at Coyle's Men's Furnishings was only meant to keep the cash flowing, the same courtesy shown anyone willing to pay for the pampering and fawning that was part of the stock in trade with the Coyle's good politics, good business. "Well, them two, Timmy and young Marshall, hadn't been getting along for some time; those damn farm kids always seem to be antagonizing our boys one way or another. It's just another example of them farmers bringing trouble as far as I'm concerned. Well, the offshoot of it was, Timmy is supposed to have said something about the little gal this Marshall fellow was with and they got into a big fight. Seems later on that night Marshall came back and found Timmy down by the Eagle's hall and beat the bejesus out of him with a pipe, killed him. As if manslaughter wasn't enough, now they're going to get him for murder."

Although the station master wanted to seem compassionate, even feeling sorry for the young man in jail, it was apparent to Tom this was the best gossip he'd had a chance to spread in a long while.

Thoughtfully, Tom returned the station master's gaze. He had listened to enough of the man's drivel and knew it was time to leave. "I'll probably get a chance to see this fellow for myself," Tom began. "You see, from what you're telling me, I think that transient, as you called him, the fellow in the snowbank, the one nobody will miss, is my brother." With that, Tom turned angrily on his heel, pulled his collar up and jammed his hat onto his head, then started the long trek to the courthouse.

CHAPTER THREE

As Tom worked his way up the long hill he wished there were a taxi in this little town. Although he preferred to walk when it made sense, right here and now it made very little sense.

The village of Montevideo had been settled on the flood plain where the Chippewa and Minnesota Rivers joined. The valley was flat and wooded, and it had been the perfect settlement for Native Americans for centuries. Dakotah and Chippewa had traded control of the valley several times before the white settlers claimed it for themselves. To early pioneers the Minnesota River had been a perfect highway into the hilly wilderness.

As the little community expanded, the plateaus to the east and west were joined to the valley businesses by a myriad of roadways climbing up the steep valley walls. The Third Street hill, up which Tom was now climbing, had been cut along the valley's east wall, gouged out parallel to the valley below. Tonight the arctic wind used the street as a funnel, constricting and compacting the bitter arctic cold as it crossed the plateau, dropping into the valley below, and Tom found himself trudging directly into that bone chilling wind. It made his eyes water, the tears froze to his cheeks and formed tiny ice cycles on his eye lashes. Every few minutes Tom was forced to stop and taking off his gloves he pressed the palms of his hands to his face in order to melt the ice which threatened to freeze his eyes shut. Other times he would use his warmed hands to cover his ears which felt like they were on fire, trying in vain to transfer enough body heat to save them from frost bite.

By the time he reached the courthouse Tom was in an agony of cold. The harsh wind penetrated even his warm wool coat, and his trouser legs were wet to the knees from the deep snow accumulated on the sidewalks. Even inside his rubbers, both feet were soaking wet and painfully cold.

Then, as Tom lunged against the wind, the courthouse loomed before him, dark except for dim lights coming from the jail. The somber brick building hovered forebodingly as Tom walked up the wide stairs, heading for the lone sign which announced "*SHERIFF*."

As Tom entered the dark building he realized that for the first time since he learned of Ernie's death he would soon be forced to talk about his brother. The thought caused a shiver up his back. Ernie, the brother he had loved so much, who had not been just a brother, but the only father he could recall. Soon, he would claim his brother, who would be put on the train and escorted home to Marion, to be buried in the family plot beside his father. As Tom's footsteps echoed in the quiet hall he knew it would not be his brother he would soon claim, but the shell, the gray package which had been Ernie's home for all these years. He knew Ernie had already made the trip home, and even now as he was preparing himself for his unpleasant task, Tom knew Ernie's spirit was already with his family in Ohio. This was to be just a formal exercise, the final declaration of Tom's love for his brother.

Before he left this town, however, Tom thought he would like to see the man who killed his brother. He wanted to look into the eyes of the man who was responsible for Ernie's death. "How could he do it, just drive off and leave him? Stranger or not, any man deserves more than that," he thought.

Tom's heels echoed loudly now on the hard tile floor as he walked toward the sheriff's office. Beyond the door he could hear coarse laughter as the sheriff and his deputies enjoyed some private humor. Tom stopped for a moment at the door and took the worn telegram from his inside pocket. Slowly he unfolded and read it once more, then stepped inside the office.

"Sheriff, I'm Tom Hall," he began, as he entered the room, "from Marion, Ohio. You probably got my telegram. We got yours." His gaze quickly covered the three men in the room as he offered the telegram to the sheriff, then continued, "I'd liked to make arrangements now, if I can, to get my brother's body shipped home."

Without waiting for a response Tom blurted, "Before I go however, I understand that you've got in your jail the man who hit my brother with his car then drove off and left him to die beside the road. Sheriff, before I go I'd like to see this man. I'd like to see what kind of man it takes to kill another and leave him there. When I get Ernie's body home I'd like to be able to tell my mother about the man who's sitting in your jail, charged not only with manslaughter, but as I understand, now charged also with the murder of another man." Tom had not realized until this moment how deep his anger was. From the moment he had learned of Ernie's death he had sensed an enormous loss and he had been deeply melancholy as his train carried him westward to this meeting. But now, because of the joviality he had barged in to, he felt only anger. "What kind of man is this, Sheriff?"

Sheriff Carl Brown rolled his chair back from the desk where he'd been sitting with his feet propped next to his coffee cup. As he rose to his feet and turned to the man who'd just spoken, Tom saw before him a middle-aged man whose presence was far greater than his bulk. Not that the sheriff was a small man; like Tom, he was six feet tall, but this man was also wide. Dressed in wrinkled khaki, Carl presented a conflicting image. Everything about Carl Brown shouted "Well, ain't I just a good old boy?" To the casual observer Carl may well have seemed a large country bumpkin, but even through the wrinkled clothes Tom could see that the sheriff had massive, powerful arms that bulged against the shirt's sleeves, and the hands protruding from the sleeves were like large firm hams. No, inside the wrinkled uniform Tom saw a powerful man, and Tom noticed everything about the sheriff smiled except his eyes. The dark eyes that measured Tom in a glance appeared hard and calculating in this otherwise cherubic face. Something in Tom shuddered a warning.

"It's a pleasure to meet you, Mr. Hall. I'm sorry it's under these circumstances. Yeah, you're right," the sheriff continued. "We've got that fellow in jail again." He hitched his black service belt into place, tucked in his shirt. Tom watched as the sheriff's huge arms pressed against the khaki sleeves. "It seems like once these fellows get started on a crooked path there's no turning them around."

"You know," Carl continued, "when these kids come off the farm they think they're God Almighty. They come charging into town, and if one of them gets lucky enough to find a job, to take one away from one of our boys from town, they just lord it all over them." He smiled slightly as he quickly glanced at the telegram before handing it back. "....try to let the world know they're something special, if you know what I mean."

As the two men shook hands now, Carl began to apply a subtle extra pressure, squeezing Tom's hand only enough to establish his own dominance. To his surprise, the young man responded in kind, with a firm but unaggressive grip of his own. Tom replied, "I know what you mean, Sheriff." Carl Brown wondered what that meant.

"It's a little unorthodox to let you see the man, Mister Hall, but since you're going to be heading back east and all, I guess it's the least I can do. You just follow me down the hall and I'll introduce you to the man who killed your brother."

As he reached for the keys hanging on a peg above his desk Carl again apprised the younger man who had come through the door to the sheriff's office to retrieve his brother's body. He wondered just how much Tom Hall was going to want to know before he headed back to Ohio. "Was it going to be a mistake to show Tom Hall the sheriff's special guest? Nah! Damn city slickers! He'll just have a look at him, get it out of his system, then I'll arrange for him to get his brother's body and he'll be on his way. By tomorrow I reckon he'll be on his way back east and I'll be rid of him once and for all."

CHAPTER
FOUR
January 29, 1938

"Sometimes," Ernie thought as he walked through the heavy snow, "even payday isn't enough to make this job worth staying on." As the winter became more severe, more confining, living at the Lac Qui Parle work camp had become increasingly difficult for Ernie. Now it wasn't just the weather. Other factors were also coming into play.

Ernie had been on this job since 1936, one of the first men hired to work on the WPA dam project. He had been fired twice from the project but hired back again because when all was said and done, he was a good worker. He was older than most of the men on the project and more reliable as well. Although he enjoyed a cold beer now and then, no one could remotely consider him a drinker. He never missed a minute of work because of a drinking binge or a hangover which was more than could be said for many of the other men.

He had lost nearly two months of work that time in the winter of 1936, however, when one of the horses on the team he was driving got spooked by an owl that flew up from a brush pile. He hadn't been driving the team for long, he recalled. He should have known better, or, he should have just been more careful. The season's first snow had fallen overnight, and his team was skittish as they worked deeper into the woods. They seemed to have forgotten they had followed the same skid road for weeks. Perhaps, it was the clumps of snow sliding from the warming evergreens that continued to thump loudly around them that kept the horses nervous. In any case, when it happened, his reactions had been too slow, and he paid the price.

From a snow covered brush pile the huge owl had leaped, thrashing its great wings to become airborne. The owl's mouse-colored summer feathers had been replaced by a beautiful mantle of white, interspersed with an occasional black feather, and the sudden white flurry turned Ernie's team into nearly two tons of screaming nightmare as they leaped and pawed the air, frightened senseless by the unexpected bird.

When the team bolted Ernie had was thrown off balance, slammed into a huge elm, before being thrown to the ground and dragged through the woods. The two huge gray geldings ran only a short distance before they became tangled in brush, but Ernie had taken a muscle tearing ride, fortunate in the end not to have had the log he was skidding or one of the huge horses crush him in the scramble. As it was, they'd had to amputate what remained of two of Ernie's fingers, which had been crushed, and mangled too badly to save. His shoulder and elbow hurt like hell ever since. Like a living barometer now, when a storm approached, Ernie's bones ached.

In addition to that, living in this hellhole camp for forty-four dollars a week, forty-three dollars and ninety-six cents to be exact, was becoming unbearable. He wasn't sure he'd stick it out until spring.

As he trudged through the snow Ernie recalled how he had come to be here. It had been a long trek from back east. The trip from Marion, Ohio, to Watson, Minnesota, had been very long; indeed, not only in miles, but in long days and nights in strange, lonely places. Day by day he drifted further from home by way of Cleveland, and then Gary, Indiana, and Chicago, then St. Louis, and then St. Paul in 1933, '34, and '35. There had been a hundred small towns whose names he had long ago forgotten.

There had just been no work around the steel and rubber towns after the big stock market crash, Ernie recalled. For a long while he had tried to get by in Marion, but finally he had to admit there was just no work to be found anywhere in the area and he had begun to drift. As much as he hated it, he said goodbye to his mother, and promising to write, he had headed west in search of employment. The depression had taken its toll on working men all across the country, and everywhere Ernie went it was the same, no work.

In the beginning there was a certain excitement. He was always on the move, visiting places which had only been names and pictures to him. For a while it seemed like recapturing part of his youth, camping out, walking along strange rivers, watching fiery sunrises. It was the boyhood he never had growing up in a poor steel town.

Eventually the shine went off. Cold mornings without a meal or days of rain spent huddling in a culvert or in an unused entrance to some empty building in another angry town began to bring back memories of his mother's loving smile, the fresh bread, the smell of clean sheets which he hadn't touched for months.

Many days on end Ernie had walked along the highway, not sure where he was going to spend the night. "How many nights," he wondered "had he just laid down in the ditch or in a farm grove or a barn and slept?" When the sun rose each day he just resumed the pattern of the previous day; put one foot in front of the other until you get someplace and until something happens.

He caught a ride on railroad boxcars a couple of times, but somehow he always felt as if his life was in jeopardy when riding the rails. The hobo jungles along the lonely tracks were not only depressing, but filled with feral men, shifty eyes looking askance at him. Ernie was sure if one of them didn't kill him for his jacket or shoes it would be the railroad bulls, the police, who would corner him in a boxcar, as they had some others, and beat him to death. "No," he thought, "it was better to follow the highways, taking the chance he'd find a job, a day's work that would save him from just one cold and hungry night." So, day after hopeless day Ernie walked west, and occasionally he found enough work to keep himself out of the soup lines. And every day found him further from his home.

Before landing this job in western Minnesota, Ernie had accepted jobs he never thought he'd tackle. In Chicago one fall he'd worked as a hod carrier on a WPA building, a school he recalled now, carrying mortar up for brick layers until he thought his back and legs couldn't climb another ladder rung.

One summer he had swept streets by hand in a little Wisconsin town, and in South St. Paul, he worked in the stockyards for a while. There he did everything from disemboweling cattle to shoveling cow shit into huge manure wagons. He worked twelve hour shifts in the cattle yards, six days a week. The stench of hot guts and blood and the smell of urine and manure permeated every pore of his tired body. He'd about reached the end of the line with that job when, in May of 1936, he heard about the big flood control project starting out by Watson, a little burg about a hundred-fifty miles away. Relying on some intuition which told him things eventually had to get better he hitched a ride on top of a Milwaukee Road cattle car a few nights later, and arrived in Montevideo, a rich man with four dollars in his pocket. The next day he walked the eleven miles to the dam project.

The change that took place in Ernie was instantaneous. Montevideo was a little farm town nestled in a long deep valley. The town was surrounded by rolling prairies and dotted here and there with small farms which were in turn surrounded by great groves of trees that were just beginning to step forth in their new spring coats of green.

This was the land where the Minnesota River and the Chippewa River came together. The soil was rich and the entire countryside had a fresh and welcoming smell. It was a new world here, and it was welcoming Ernie as no place he had seen since leaving home. Even as he was careful to steer clear of the railroad yards, moving furtively in the shadows as he left town, Ernie couldn't help feeling energized. "This is great country," he thought as he left the town behind and walked north in the warm spring sunshine. For a boy from the city, this sparsely populated country of Minnesota seemed like paradise.

In good years, the Minnesota River Valley and other small valleys which joined it were indeed paradise, and now the rich farmland was just coming green after a long winter. Along the two rivers, great forests of oaks and elms grew as they had for centuries. A hundred years before Ernie walked through the valley the Dakotah and Chippewa Indians had called this place *from-a-mount-I-see*; Montevideo, in the English language, or simply Monte to the local people.

Even before the Indians populated the valleys of the Minnesota River, there had been bison and deer as well as elk and wolves and a multitude of other wild game that called this area home since the end of the last great ice age. And from the very beginning all the residents here shared a common link. In the spring of the year, when the snow and ice melted, the Minnesota River flooded the adjoining valleys from its headwaters sixty miles north at Bigstone Lake, to the point where, after wriggling through a couple of hundred miles of countryside, the Minnesota joined the great Mississippi River on the opposite side of the state. The floods had been a fact to be lived with for eons. In the spring the river that provided so well during the remainder of the year overflowed its banks, filling a thousand square miles of forests and farms and towns with cold, silt laden water, destroying all that stood in the way of its raging torrents.

But now, in the twentieth century, farmers and engineers alike, realized that civilization needed to control the river's wild temperament. In the period between 1903 and 1920 alone, the mighty Minnesota River had overflowed its banks sixteen times and caused millions of dollars of damage.

By 1920 surveys were complete, determining how and where the Minnesota River could be controlled and in January, 1936, President Roosevelt gave a final approval to Works Progress Administration, the WPA, Project Number 2484. The largest flood control project ever completed in Minnesota would begin before 1936 came to an end.

When project 2484 was complete, in 1938, the flooding waters of four rivers, the Chippewa, Lac Qui Parle, Pomme de Terre, and the Minnesota River would finally be controlled, and the newly created Lac Qui Parle Lake's depth would be thirteen feet deep, in effect, creating a new lake some thirty five miles long and in some places three miles wide.

Ernie Hall was not thinking of this; however. He didn't care that the Lac Qui Parle Project as it was labeled, would provide several years of employment for this rural area. He was only hoping to find honest work to sustain him and eventually get him home once more.

At the age of forty-six, Ernie found he was getting tired. *Yes, this old boy is wearing out*, he thought from time to time. It seemed sometimes, that he had already worked a lifetime.

He had been just nineteen when his dad died and he had become the family's breadwinner whether he planned to or not. Somehow though, Ernie had never felt unjustly burdened. It had come to him naturally. Baby Tom had become more than a brother to him, and although Ernie kidded Tom about being old enough to be his father, he sometimes actually found himself thinking of Tom as his son.

Like father and son, they had grown through the years together. From a toddler to a young man graduating from high school, Ernie had been Tom's provider, his confidant, protector, and pal. When Tom and Ernie and their mother joined hands in Thanksgiving prayer, the love he felt for them made his heart swell. He always blamed the catch in his voice at those moments on the dry air or his collar being too tight, but suspected they knew the real cause.

Ernie had felt especially proud the day Tom went off to college. Ernie had known from the start; he wasn't cut out for college himself; he was a working man and knew it. But it made Ernie proud to know he had made it possible for Tom to finish four years at Ohio State, then go on to get a Navy commission when he was twenty-four years old. If his memory served him right, Tom should be home from the Navy for good sometime this year. Like a father, Ernie wondered what Tom would do when he got back to Marion.

Ernie walked at a comfortable but purposeful pace from Montevideo. When he was younger he would have attacked this country at a faster pace, getting to his destination in the shortest time he could, but now he took time to enjoy his surroundings. Sometimes he did feel like he was just wearing out. He sometimes found himself dreaming of the pleasant days so long in the past.

If anyone had told Ernie he was homesick he would have denied it; and believed the denial himself if no one else did. An entire lifetime had been sacrificed to provide for his family, and as he passed through the verdant farmlands here Ernie was finally and unequivocally alone, nearing the end of an arduous journey.

At the relaxed pace he set, Ernie still had reached the Lac Qui Parle Dam project in just over a half day, even with a stop where he splurged on lunch in the little village called Watson. After a short rest in a grove at the edge of town, Ernie had walked the last four miles in just over an hour. As he crested the hill above the river he smiled as he looked out over the vast wooded valley a half mile below him.

All across the valley he saw a huge forest of elms, box elders and oaks which surrounded the river. The trees drifted in green waves up the small adjoining valleys. For a moment Ernie thought he caught the smell of fresh baked bread.

The gravel road he followed now wound downhill, curving northward for a short way before crossing the river. The Minnesota River at this time of the year filled its banks and flowed beneath a wooden trestle, designed more for horses pulling wagons than for the automobiles, which were seen more frequently, here in the farm country. A half mile or so upstream Ernie could see in the afternoon light the old concrete dam with its spillway, which was too low to be functional in flood control and would be replaced over the next two years.

Ernie carried all his earthly belongings in a bundle across his back as he searched for the construction office, hoping this journey would not prove to be in vain, and for the first time since leaving Ohio, Ernie felt like he was coming home.

CHAPTER
FIVE

Ernie found that competition for the jobs here on the project was tough. Although the initial workforce was shortly to number close to three hundred men, there were a lot of local men who wanted to work, and priority seemed to go to them. Ernie knew he was qualified under the welfare program administered by the WPA, but he was a stranger here. He was a long way from home, and his record of having quit several jobs didn't do him any good when his name came up in the hiring line.

Ernie hung around the work camp for a week before the crew boss threw him an axe one morning and yelled at him to get his ass on the flat bed wagon for the ride into the woods. It was the break he needed, had waited for, and for the next several months Ernie worked in the woods with axe and saw, cutting the elm, cottonwood, and box elder needed for building the camp and for shoring at the dam site.

Ernie had been told there had been big wood cutting projects around Lac Qui Parle Lake since 1934, but since the project had now officially begun, the cutting was being done in earnest. Six days a week the crews went into the woods. Sometimes they worked close in and sometimes they cut wood several miles away, leaving before sunrise in order to get in a full day's cutting.

Ernie found the demanding physical work to his liking, and for the first time in months his enthusiasm for life came back. It was much better to work like this than to be trapped in mission soup lines or fighting for survival in the hobo jungles at the edge of towns all across the country. For the first time in years, since he'd left Ohio, he found a place that felt like home, and he liked the farmland around him more each day.

When he wasn't cutting wood he liked to walk the countryside, to wave at a young man cultivating corn or to lend a willing hand to the old man trying to stretch his fence tight again after his calves had pushed it over. And for the first time since he left home he met people who were not on the move. He met the farmers and the mailman and the farrier who made his circuit among the farms trimming and shoeing the vast number of huge draft horses still needed to work the farms of the valley.

Although most of the workers at the camp felt alienated from the local residents, were looked down upon, sneered at because they were "transients," Ernie made friends and became a familiar face at many of the area farms as well as in Watson and Milan. There was something the locals saw in Ernie that was different— maybe even permanent. He seemed to belong in the valley.

Occasionally now, Ernie found himself invited to Sunday dinner at some neighborhood farm home. Once everyone got past the discomfort of being strangers, they found they had many things in common, and the time passed rapidly as they swapped their stories.

On one of his trips into the woods Ernie had passed the remains of deserted buildings, a collection of weathered grey lumber and stone rubble lying in disarray back in the woods along the river not far north of the construction site. He asked his host about the ruins one Sunday. "I've wondered," he said, "about that old foundation in the woods. When we went up past

Brendemoen's farm to cut wood I could see it off along the river but have never gotten down there to have a closer look. It seems to me it's a strange place for farm buildings, hardly a good place for livestock."

"You're probably talking about the old fort, just a ways in the woods by the old mission." His host was more than willing to share the story. "Isn't it strange," he continued. "Nobody gives that place a thought anymore."

"Most of the folks around here have already forgotten about the old fort. I suppose that's natural; even out here change takes place, you know. I guess by the time my grandchildren take over this farm no one will even know there was a fort here."

"When I was a boy," he continued, "part of it was still standing, but the fort itself has been empty nearly a hundred years and it's just been neglected for a long time."

"Back in the 1820's there used to be a stockade there, Ernie; just below where the road is now. The stockade was built by a fellow named Joseph Renville. You couldn't know of course, but the Minnesota River used to be a real river highway for the trappers and the Indians."

"Well, Renville was part Indian, you see, Sioux, or Dakotah, as they're known. They say his mother was married to a French fur trader who came up this way from St. Paul. Renville was a pretty unique fellow. He got an education and then, would you believe it, he fought with the British in the War of 1812! After that he went to work for the Hudson's Bay Company, and then a few years later he helped set up the American Fur Company out here on the river. That outfit gave Hudson's Bay quite a run for a while, especially when that big money fellow, John Jacob Astor, went into partnership with them some years later, but that's another story."

"Well, this was quite a place around here at that time, I guess. Renville set himself up like a king, they say. There were lots of travelers through this area in those days; explorers, trappers, settlers, and the like."

"They used to bring those big ox carts through here on their way up to Pembina, too. That's up in Canada. There are some places in the woods where you can still see the tracks that they made, and that was a hundred years ago. Just imagine, those big carts with their huge wheels creaking so they could be heard from a mile away. Eventually I suppose the tracks will disappear too, and then everyone will just forget this used to be just wilderness."

"Renville was responsible for bringing in the first missionaries too. The Jesuits built that log cabin you see back in the woods there. I suppose it was because he was part Indian himself, that he helped the missionaries translate the bible and hymn books into Dakotah. That's their language you know and it had never been written down until the Jesuits took on the task."

"Well, things change sometimes without our wanting them to, and it was no different for Renville. In the 1830's they had a run of crop failures around here, just like we've had recently, and Renville lost everything he had. He died a dozen or so years later without a penny. I always thought it was a crime that all the people Renville helped make millionaires just ignored him when he needed them."

Over the months Ernie shared his stories as well, becoming a welcome guest rather than just one of the transients.

During the week Ernie occasionally traded in his axe for a shovel or a pick and he worked on the road which would eventually service the dam. Even with the modern dump trucks and caterpillar tractors it was a big job. When the new dam was in place, the road which would cross over its bridge top would be half a mile south of its previous location and elevated on a dike running across the entire valley. Although it would mean little to Ernie, the old dam, and the bridge, upstream in the Minnesota River would be removed and little Lac Qui Parle Lake would someday swell to cover over forty-seven square miles.

That winter, 1936, Ernie had a chance to take over a team of horses, skidding logs from the woods most days and some days operating a drag to level the roadbed. Even though the big diesel caterpillars worked well and moved massive amounts of dirt, teams of horses were still the mainstay of the construction force. Ernie took to driving a team immediately. He liked the huge sweaty bulk of his team of gray geldings that responded to his deep gentle voice.

When he'd had the accident in the woods Ernie feared it was all over, that he might lose his job. They'd wanted to take Ernie's team from him after the accident, had in fact given the team to Ollie Martin while Ernie was laid up from his injuries. As it turned out however, while Ollie could handle most of the tasks he'd been called upon to do, he was totally unsuited to working with horses and the project manager wasted no time putting Ernie back with his team as soon as he was healed enough to manage them, and that was the beginning of the bad times for Ernie.

Ollie Martin resented losing what he saw as a sweet job to Ernie. Driving that team had given Ollie's ego the boost it had needed, and he blamed Ernie, when that sweet job was taken away and given back to Ernie. Ollie was twenty-nine years old, almost twenty years younger than Ernie. Ollie had worked construction most of his life and although he wasn't the only bully on the dam job, he was certainly a man to stay clear of. It was no mistake when men said he was hard as nails. Neither was it a stretch to say his mood was always mean and ugly. More than one man had failed to return to work after fighting with Ollie.

Now Ollie Martin was seeking revenge over his lost job, and he was making the already miserable winter unbearable for Ernie. At every opportunity Ollie tried to provoke Ernie into a fight, a fight Ernie wasn't sure he could win. Spilling his coffee on Ernie in the mess hall, dropping firewood on him as he passed in the barracks, slapping too hard Ernie's bad shoulder in mock friendship were only Ollie's more subtle challenges.

Worse for Ernie were the paydays, when all the boys would gather for a couple of drinks. With those few drinks fueling his resentment Ollie was especially hard to deal with. His anger seemed to fester like a boil which could only be lanced by attacking Ernie. After Ollie had a few drinks Ernie tried hard to stay out of his way. Any place that Ollie was not was the place Ernie wanted to be on paydays.

Knowing that if he stayed away from Ollie his life in the camp would be that much easier Ernie usually sought other places to relax. If he thought Ollie was across the road at Buster's, he would walk the nearly four miles to the municipal in Watson, or he would walk the shorter distance to Lac Qui Parle Village, which everyone these days called Pinch town since it was just a little pinch of a town. They all laughed at that.

pinch town was up on the hill west of the site, just a little over three miles away. There was a little 3.2 beer joint up there that wasn't too bad for a drink. On Sundays there was a crowd from nearby Boyd and Canby that came to pinch town for their drinking and entertainment. They'd started coming to pinch town during the heart of prohibition when they came to get moonshine from one of the Pedersen boys, and continued coming now, making the little town boisterous and crowded on the weekend. But it was a tough crowd that gathered there and in general they didn't like the men from the transient camp. In addition, it was a hard walk through all the construction and through the bottomland woods, full of mosquitoes in the summer and full of deep snow drifts in the winter.

Like most of the boys, Ernie preferred Watson, and like the others who liked to go into Watson, Ernie preferred to go to this little farm town's municipal liquor store or to Arnie's pool hall rather than Pinch town's single 3.2 tavern. Although the camaraderie was great in pinch town, sometimes a man just needed a little room for himself after living and working with the same men all week.

Although it had been snowing and blowing all day, it was Watson that Ernie was heading for on this Saturday. But first a beer or two at Buster's after supper had sounded good to Ernie, Ollie Martin, or no Ollie Martin. If he'd known they would be his last, the last beers he would ever drink, Ernie would have stayed at Buster's a little longer and just called it a night, just going back to the barracks instead of leaving on foot for

Watson. Tonight's four mile walk into Watson was going to be shortened to less than one mile for Ernie.

CHAPTER

SIX

Tom followed the sheriff through the heavy steel outer door to the cell block then paused as the sheriff locked the door behind them. The echo of the hard grating key sounded a counterpoint to the returning echo of the closing door. Then the two men continued down the hall, rounding the corner to ascend the steps to the cell block.

"Yes sir, I'll show this fellow how we treat law breakers here, and then he'll go home," the sheriff thought. "You can bet I'm not going to tell him everything, however. There are some things I know about this whole case nobody else needs to know. We'll just send this fellow back to Ohio. Then I'll take care of our friend Warren."

Carl saw himself as a man in charge of his own destiny. He was a man in control, and he kept abreast of what happened around him and acted accordingly. Since arriving in the valley five years ago Carl had been quietly cataloging the area's residents. Carl, like all the great generals he had studied, knew he needed to have his finger on the pulse of the community, to be aware of the cold as well as the hot spots in order to keep the law functioning smoothly. Carl knew the troublemakers, the newsmakers and the weak citizens who needed his firm guidance. To Carl control came from understanding how the merchants, the farmers, the transients, and the Indians from the area lived their lives and which of them needed his control at what time. No one was immune to the oversight of the sheriff.

Although Buster's Roadhouse, across from the dam-site project, had never been a real hot spot requiring immediate reprisals, it had been a bone of contention for Sheriff Carl Brown for most of his tenure here. If it wasn't some damn farmer brats drinking too much beer and cheap booze up there, terrorizing the town boys, badgering them into fights, it was the good for nothing transients working on that new dam project that made this part of the job a pain in the ass. Ball-Buster's, they were starting to call the little roadhouse down by the river. There seemed to always be somebody trying to bust somebody's balls out there.

In fact, Buster's Roadhouse was becoming something of a grand-scale gathering house, especially when compared to its humble beginnings. Buster had turned out to be a progressive entrepreneur.

Several years earlier, long before the building of the dam had begun, Buster had put up a little shack along the road near the Minnesota River. All he planned to do was earn a few extra nickels or dimes selling minnows to the fishermen who liked to fish in the lazy current of the river which, in many places, passed within a hundred yards or so of the road. Before Buster put up his shack they had to bring their minnows from Watson or Montevideo, and usually lost a substantial portion of them when the water in their minnow buckets became brackish while making the long slow drive to the river. Buster was able to go out to any of several creeks close by and seine minnows; he brought back shiners, chubs, and suckers, keeping them in a cold well in the little shack, nice and fresh for the eager fishermen.

There were several good holes in the river where a man could catch a limit of northern pike, and sometimes a couple of nice walleyes while spending a relaxing day away from town, in the woods where it was peaceful and quiet. It was also possible to fish in Lac Qui Parle Lake, just a couple of miles up-river from Buster's, but to get into the lake it was necessary to cross through one of the many farms surrounding the lake, then follow through the often muddy trails to the lake. It was also possible to get onto the lake at the little resort on the west side of the lake, but most were content to fish from the Bushman Bridge just north of Buster's shack or at one of the still pools along the river.

Buster found that the fishermen were more than happy to buy their bait from him. Even those who were going further south along the river to fish the wide slow moving stretch below the Stay Bridge found it advantageous to detour the couple of miles to Buster's rather than bring their bait from Montevideo. It wasn't so much the cost of the lost minnows as it was the inconvenience of not having the fresh bait available when needed that made Buster's bait shack a popular stop.

Eventually, Buster began keeping sodas and candy bars on hand, and soon he built a larger building where he offered lunches and beer. Now, after just a couple of years, Buster's had become a regular attraction, and for Carl, which was the problem. These days it attracted not only the fishermen, but especially on weekends it attracted the farmers' kids and those damn transient workers who were building the new damn and who lived in the big camp across the road from Buster's.

Carl really hated those damn transients. All those bastards did, it seemed to Carl, was drink and fight. And try to screw all the women in town. You could hardly go to Watson these days without seeing two or three drunken asshole transients there. On the weekends, when they'd been paid, they were all over the place, sleeping in the ditches when it was warm and God only knows where they slept when it got cold.

Carl didn't know which he hated more, the farmers or the transients. One thing he did know, however, was that he'd take no crap from either one, and that the only thing he hated more than farmers and transients was those damn drunken Indians.

When it came to Indians Carl was adamant; "Those assholes cost me my last job." Carl was not hesitant to let his feelings about Indians be known. It had cost him his job when he shot one of the Indian men in Yellow Medicine County a couple of years ago. "That lousy bastard tried to stop me from screwing one of the squaws. Damn worthless buck thought he was somebody important, he did, not just a fucking Indian." It made his blood boil. "It wasn't even his own squaw. Besides, that's all them damn squaws wanted. They want to come to town, drink until they fall down, then fuck whoever came by; assholes."

Carl Alan Brown had shown up in Granite Falls, the Yellow Medicine County seat, for the first time anyone could remember on a Saturday night. His self-introduction to the community was to be but a preview of things to come, and those present that Saturday had cause to remember him clearly.

While no one could recall hearing exactly where Carl Brown came from, after that night they were constantly aware of his presence throughout the county. Few people were brave enough to think of asking Carl's life history.

A little before midnight Carl had entered the Granite Bar. Just a half block up from the Minnesota River, and at the lower end of Main Street, the Granite Bar was a dive, a pollutant to the otherwise pious and tidy community. The Granite Bar was, along with its other shortcomings, the only place in this little self-righteous town which frequently preached forward while practicing backward, where the young men from the Sioux Indian Agency just outside of town could buy illicit moonshine.

Carl was trying to squeeze between the chairs of two revelers when one such man from the Agency, Harold Crow, after a long day of trying to eke out a living from his rock poor farm along the river had backed from the storeroom with a precious pint of liquor in his back pocket. Unaware of Carl's presence, Harold Crow grazed Carl's shoulder as he turned to make his way to the door. Instantly enraged, Carl attacked the unsuspecting man.

With a vicious shove Carl rammed Harold Crow into the row of occupied stools at the bar, spilling several drinks in the process. As the surprised man fought to gain his balance Carl drove a boot into his side then viciously continued to press his advantage. The attack had come so unexpectedly that Harold Crow was still not sure what was happening except that for some reason, he was being badly assaulted. He threw up his hands to protect against a blow he was sure would be aimed at his head, but as he did, Carl instead kicked him in the groin. Then, as he folded in pain Carl attacked again with his fists. There was no contest. In moments, Harold Crow was forced out into the street by Carl and in a final flurry of rage Carl lifted him up by the collar and belt, throwing him violently against a parked car before he spoke for the first time, brief and to the point. "Keep your smelly red hide out of my sight." The remainder of the night Carl spent explaining to the Granite Bar's crowd how he thought Indians needed to be handled.

On Monday morning Carl strode into the office of the Yellow Medicine County Sheriff. The tale of his Saturday encounter preceded him, and within the half hour Carl Brown wore the uniform and badge of deputy sheriff.

In the following months Carl's reputation in the county spread rapidly. His penchant for violent action kept even the county's more outrageous bullies in check and after the first short flurry of bent noses and cracked ribs Yellow Medicine County settled peacefully into summer complacency.

Carl's rules of deportment toward a county sheriff's deputy were simple: "keep your mouth shut and keep the goddamn Indians out of my way." There seemed to be only one exception to Carl's rule. Although he slept around with several of the community's women, Carl had a particular appetite for the women of the Sioux Agency.

Sunday was Carl's night out, his night to prowl the county bars for his own entertainment. By his own admission, a man sometimes had to get out and "howl at the moon," as he put it. Sunday was his day, and on Sundays his big black Studebaker coupe was frequently seen flying across the county's roads or parked by a tavern in Boyd, or Wood Lake, or Hazel Run, to mention only a few of his Sunday haunts. He had one steadfast rule; he never drank at the bars in Granite Falls, although at the end of his shift he sometimes escorted one of the local barmaids to his apartment.

If the white population around Granite Falls were pleased to have Carl's hard brand of justice in the county, the native population did not share their enthusiasm. At the slightest provocation, Carl invoked his hard justice. Any Indian seen drinking was fair game for Carl's night stick; whenever he saw one of the few automobiles owned by Agency residents, it was certain to be pulled over, searched, and its driver rousted about even slapped around on general principal.

The ignominious end of Carl's iron rule as a deputy came, ironically, at the Granite Bar.

Carl had broken his first rule that night; it was the first and last time he would succumb to the temptation to drink in Granite Falls. As he had driven past the Granite Bar earlier that evening he had spotted Margarita as she entered with several others. Margarita and Carl were occasional lovers; when Carl was in the mood and Margarita could slip away from her husband.

Margarita was tall, athletic, and a sexual carnivore nearly Carl's match in bed. She was also half Indian; her mother had been a little Irish Catholic girl from nearby Clara City who had fallen in love with a handsome young man from the Agency. When she ran off with him her parents turned their backs, refused to acknowledge their marriage, and she lived with the young man long enough to bear him a daughter before committing suicide by leaping into the icy river one night.

Now, thirty years later, her only child, Margarita, was unhappily married to a hardworking, but unexciting man of mixed Chippewa and Sioux blood. Her greatest pleasure came when his job on a railroad crew kept him away from home and she could enjoy the parties and good times to be found by her in Granite Falls.

Sometimes when she woke in the mornings it took a few minutes to remember where she has spent the night, and more frequently now the morning headaches and churning stomach were appeased only by another drink, but at that, it was better than waking up in her cold boring cabin by herself or to find her husband snoring on the other side of the bed.

If Carl was aware of her promiscuity he didn't seem to care. "Hell, she's not my wife; she's just a great piece of ass. If her stupid husband can't handle her he deserves it," was Carl's attitude. Occasionally, on Sunday nights, she and Carl found their way to his apartment, when all the bars had closed. Carl was never seen with Margarita or any of the Indian women in the Granite Falls bars, however. It would have been demeaning, undermining his position in the community; however, picking up a woman in one of the out of town bars was, by this standard, perfectly acceptable.

But when Carl had spotted Margarita tonight he couldn't shake her image; he was just plain horny, and Margarita was just about the best lay in the whole damn county, he thought. Carl had categorized every woman in the county who was available. Eventually he cut short his tour of the county and parking his Studebaker in the shadows he slipped in the rear entrance of the Granite Bar.

After a short quiet conversation, the bartender produced for Carl a coke laced with his private stock of moonshine. Carl was surprised at how fast and easy it when down, ordered another. He was half-way through his fourth drink when he turned to face Margarita for the first time, finding her at a corner table with a mixed group of Indian men and women. As Carl moved to a separate table he motioned with his eyes for her to join him. But, to his chagrin Margarita turned from him, looking instead to one of the men at her table.

Unused to being ignored by anyone, let alone some damn Indian, Carl found it hard to keep his temper in check. He seemed to have forgotten he was not in one of his remote haunts, but right at home in Granite Falls. Soon, like a breeding bull teased and frustrated by a group of boys some part of his brain turned off, and with still another drink adding fuel to his anger he could think only that he wanted to breed the hot blooded Margarita, and that the Indians at her table were responsible for her reluctance in joining him.

Even in the dim light of the tavern the red anger in Carl's eyes was visible as he crossed the room. Drunken frustration made the sweat stand out on Carl's face; he heard the wind roar in his head as he clamped his huge hand around Margarita's dark wrist. "God damn it, I want you to come with me!" The anger in his deep baritone voice boomed filling the room with his rage. As he yanked Margarita to her feet the others at the table cringed back, partly in fear of Carl's temper. The man at her side however voiced his protest, not realizing the foolishness of his interference.

"Sheriff," he knew Carl was in fact just a deputy, "what's this about?" Unaware that Carl and the woman were clandestine lovers, he mistakenly believed Margarita was being arrested, but could not identify the motivation. "What right do you have to do this?"

Fear showed in Margarita's eyes as Carl threw her across the room toward the table she had occupied just minutes ago. As she crashed into the table she saw Carl strike her brother-in-law with the back of his hand, then turning to face him full-on Carl's ham-like fits drove into the man's face, driving him into the heavy wood burning stove, sending chimney pipe and soot in a great clattering black cloud.

As he rose slowly from the floor events took an unfortunate turn. Dazed, disoriented by the sledgehammer blow he had taken, he reached into his jacket for his handkerchief to wipe the blood and soot from his face. Carl did not know the man's original minor resistance was now completely gone, and through his liquor jaded eyes believed his opponent was reaching for a weapon.

With a terrible roar that filled the room, "Nooooo . . ." Carl's reflexes took over, and in a smooth movement he released the safety strap, drew his .38 caliber service revolver, and began firing.

Without ever reaching his feet, Margarita's brother-in-law felt his life ebb even as the first shock waves slammed through his body. Three shots into the center of his chest from a distance of six feet drove him into the wall, wrenched his body violently into the table next to him before he collapsed. As his last life's energy drained from him a confused look came into his sad brown eyes, and tears began to streak down his cheeks. He looked at the handkerchief gripped tightly in his hand and whispered so weakly only a few were able to hear, "I don't understand, I was just reach. . ."

In spite of his protestations, Carl was forced to vacate his deputy post the following day. Enough pressure was applied, through the sheriff's office and the Agency superintendent, to keep Carl from being prosecuted but there was no longer any place in Granite Falls for Carl Brown.

CHAPTER SEVEN

It wasn't long however before Carl made the right connections in Montevideo, the county seat of Chippewa county. When the previous sheriff decided to call it quits in favor of more fishing time, Carl was at the right place at the right time. He easily explained the Yellow Medicine County incident to the Chippewa County board and the majority of its members, who wanted a sheriff with an eye on discipline rather than fishing, appointed Carl Brown to protect the county's residents.

Carl made a point of checking out Buster's every Saturday night. Buster was always good for a couple of free drinks. It was the good stuff for him, too. It was still illegal to sell hard liquor around here, although everyone including Carl had a bootlegger he could call on. And nearly everyone who was a regular around Buster's knew that Buster could find them a bottle when it was needed. Carl was smart enough to realize there was no future in arresting Buster; "that would be something like cutting off your nose to spite your face," Carl thought.

Carl liked to sit at the end of the bar, unobtrusively he thought, nursing a Coca Cola laced with moonshine and watch the girls shake their cute little asses for the boys. Most evenings the roadhouse was quiet, the girl-watching satisfactory. Once in a while on Saturday night he'd see a couple, all huggy-face, slip out into the night. Carl would smile, knowing they'd be rattling the windows of their car before long, screwing their brains out. It gave him a charge when he figured they were all tangled up like angleworms in a can, to move quietly alongside the car, then shine his big five cell flashlight on them and watch them scramble for something to cover up with. Once last summer he'd gotten extra lucky. He caught one of the girls, bare ass naked, her ass right up in the air, giving her boyfriend a blow job. He hadn't shined his flashlight right away that night; that time he almost got his own rocks off.

But most often after he had sampled Buster's liquor Carl just liked to bully the farm boys a little bit. "Those poor bastards," he thought, "coming to town smelling of cow shit and Old Spice were really pathetic. If they weren't such a pain in the ass they would be comical." He knew they were trying to mimic the boys from town, dressed when they could afford it in the latest fashions right out of the Sears catalog. What a laugh they were. And the farmer he really liked to lean on most was Warren Marshall.

"If ever there was a shit-smelling goddamn smart ass farmer," Carl knew, "it was Warren Marshall." From the first time Carl had seen him it has been the same; Carl always felt his anger surge just at the sight of Warren. "Sure," Carl knew, "Warren worked in Monte now driving truck for Swifts, but he was, by God, a farmer from the word GO."

Warren wasn't just an ordinary smart ass. No, there was a special something about Warren that irritated Carl. Some kind of self-assurance that said, "I'm all right with the world; I know who I am and where I'm going." He never acquiesced to Carl. That set Carl's nerves on edge. There was one other thing about Warren that really pissed him off. Warren had that tight assed little bitch Jeanne Amundson hot after his nuts.

That more than any other reason was why Carl hated Warren. Warren had a calm assurance about him, no need to bluster, no need to brag, and in spite of every fault Carl saw in him, Jeanne thought the sun rose at Warren's feet.

Jeanne was a special one. From the first time Carl had seen her at the Chippewa County Fairgrounds, thoughts of Jeanne came to him at all odd moments. Carl had still been a deputy in Granite Falls, had come to the fair early during the set-up to kill some time when he was supposed to be checking out a stupid complaint about dogs chasing some goddamn farmer's sheep. He couldn't care less about the goddamn sheep.

Carl had been walking through the livestock barns. He always wondered what the girls thought as they passed through and saw the horses with their great big cocks hanging out. "Probably makes them wet their pants, wanting some of that for themselves," Carl thought. As he rounded the end of the long row of tie-stalls, Carl spotted Jeanne, giving a bath to a big Belgian gelding.

The horse and Jeanne were both drenched with water. Carl watched as Jeanne, not realizing she was under his scrutiny, continued to bathe the huge horse, hose in one hand, sponge in the other. As she bent to the soap bucket her blue jeans pulled tight across her hips, outlining her small but well-rounded figure. "Oh, God, look at that," Carl thought at the sight. Although she stood barely five feet tall, everything about the young woman was earthy and voluptuous. Her hair was auburn, cut in a Page Boy, and she had a tiny pug nose, full lips.

The splashing of the horse's bath water and her own perspiration caused Jeanne's white cotton blouse, tucked into her jeans, to cling tight against her delicate body, and as she plied the sponge back and forth across the great horse, her unhaltered breasts seemed to float, inviting Carl to devour them. For a brief instant as she turned, Carl watched the gentle curve of a breast barely exposed by an errant button at the front of her blouse before Jeanne ducked behind her bath mate.

As she turned behind the horse, Jeanne for the first time, noticed her audience, and at first only mildly embarrassed, she grabbed a towel from the chest against the wall to blot some of the water from herself. Under Carl's continued silent watch, however, she soon moved away, blushing in embarrassment and anger at the stranger's rudeness.

No matter Carl was twenty years older than Jeanne. Once she'd been laid by him, he knew, she'd never again be satisfied with that smart ass farmer Warren. Time and again he thought of Jeanne standing alongside the huge Belgian gelding; "she probably thinks of me every time she runs her hand over that big cock." He missed the irony of his foolish analogy to the gelding. "Someday I'll get a chance to show her what she's missing." Carl sometimes found himself involuntarily thinking of Jeanne even when he was in bed with another woman . . . especially when he was in bed with another woman.

CHAPTER
EIGHT

"Off your ass, Warren," the sheriff barked as he and Tom Hall passed through the final door into the cell block. "There's someone here who wants to meet you." Carl was going to enjoy showing off his prisoner. He found real satisfaction having Warren in his jail. "Take a good look at this feller, Mr. Hall. This here's the one who did it, run over your brother." The 'good-old-boy' oozed from Carl. "This is the guy that beat our Timmy Coyle to death, didn't give him a chance at all by the looks of everything back there in the alley. We don't take kindly to his kind around here, so you'll have to overlook some of the bumps he's carrying on him but it won't matter much when the judge is done with him."

Tom Hall watched as the young man, a man not much younger than himself, lifted himself gingerly off the steel bunk. "My God," Tom thought as he watched Warren struggle to his feet. "They've beat this poor guy to a pulp." For a moment he almost forgot this was the man who ran over his brother, the man who had killed Ernie and left him alongside the road.

Warren stood, leaning one hand on the bunk for support and looked at Tom. He looked like he was badly hurt. Warren's nose was broken, and both eyes were swollen, one completely shut and the other appeared to have only a minimum of vision. The way Warren held his arm around his stomach made Tom believe there might also be some broken ribs. "I wonder why they don't have him in the hospital?" he thought. At the sight of the young man Tom recalled for a moment his observations of the sheriff only minutes ago. "What in the world happened to this fellow, Sheriff?"

Carl applied his disarming smile. "He tried to resist us, the young man did. He should have come in peaceful, but oh, no. He thought he'd give us a lickin, like he did Timmy Coyle. Only there was three of us there. We had to soften him up a little before we could make him fit in the car. Come on now, you've seen him now. Let's ease on out of here. There's no reason to lose any sleep over this fellow."

"Just a minute, Sheriff. I'd like a minute or two alone with your prisoner." Tom's words were more a statement of fact than a request.

Although the request was unusual, the sheriff acknowledged Tom's need to see his brother's killer. *After all, he's come a long way to find out who killed his brother even if the son of a bitch was a goddamn transient.* For another moment, Carl considered whether he should leave this man, who had obvious reason to hate this prisoner, alone in the cell block with Warren. *The worst he can do is kill that son of a bitch,* he concluded with a smile. *But that isn't likely. What the hell.* As he passed through the door he stared hard at Tom. "It'll be locked; just yell out when you're ready."

As the sheriff's footsteps faded down the hall Tom turned his attention toward Warren. For a long while he just stood and stared at the young man in the cell. Tom's emotions were charged, confused. At one point he moved as if about to say something to the prisoner, then without having spoken a word, turned toward the door where he knew his own freedom was only a shout away.

Tom had only taken a single step when Warren hesitantly called to him. "Mister . . . . . ."

Tom turned to see Warren standing with his hands clenched tightly around the cell bars. He had tears running from his swollen eyes. "Mister, I know you've got no reason to believe me, but honest to God I didn't kill your brother." If Tom was surprised by the simple exclamation of innocence, the next words Warren spoke shook him to the core.

"I didn't kill the other fellow either." Meekly then Warren turned and sat heavily on his bunk with his head hanging between his knees.

"What are you saying, man? The sheriff told me the evidence shows clearly that you ran over my brother and left him in the snow. He also says there's absolutely no question you beat Tim Coyle to death only days after we let you out on bail. From the comments of the station master it sounds like the whole town, if not the entire county, knows how guilty you are. If you're trying to play a cruel trick on me it isn't going to work."

After this hot outburst Tom turned to leave, and again Warren spoke. Warren's eyes held a frightened plea as he continued. "I wasn't even in Monte the night Timmy Coyle was killed. And—oh sure—I had been drinking the night your brother died. I can't question that my tire tracks were found there, and that I ran over his body, but I know I didn't hit your brother . . . I never saw a soul after Jeanne and I left Buster's. Even in the storm I'm sure I would have seen your brother if he had been walking along the roadway."

"I just wouldn't do a hit and run on anybody, Mister. The only thing I can think of might be that your brother was already dead, or maybe passed out, but even then I'm sure I would have seen him unless the snow had covered him up. Man, it was blowing like crazy that night. It had been storming all day and in every protected place the snow had piled up, sometimes all the way across the road. Man, I got sober in a hurry driving in that stuff, and I wasn't even sure we were going to make it to Jeanne's place."

The meek voice that slipped from Warren's pulpy face finished, "You've got to help me mister."

Tom's thoughts raced as he turned again to the steel door. He pounded angrily twice on the heavy door. "Sheriff Brown," he barked. "Open up, I'm ready to leave."

The sheriff himself opened the door a short time later to see Tom, his face gray as he eased through to the other hall. The sheriff looked as if he was going to speak but Tom quickly interjected "I guess it was just too much for my nerves to look at the guy who ran over my brother. He sure doesn't look like a murderer, but then, I guess one just doesn't know, does one?" All Tom wanted now was to get out of the jail, to be back in the fresh air.

"I'm going to be around for a couple of days making arrangements for my brother, Sheriff. When does this fellow come to trial?"

"Well Mr. Hall, I think the court date has been set for about two weeks. The hit and run on your brother is an open and shut case as far as I'm concerned, and it looks like it's going to be a murder charge, too. We've got the iron bar he used on Coyle, and I don't think it'll take more than a few days to put this fellow away for keeps."

"I may stick around to see that." As Tom spoke, he watched the sheriff out of the corner of his eye and saw Carl blanch, his eyes widening for an instant.

Unconsciously, the sheriff snapped and unsnapped the safety strap over his service revolver.

"No need for you to do that, son," the wind roared in his ears as the sheriff calmly responded, "You know, we don't get too many of his kind around here, but we do know how to take care of them. It seems to be he's caused you enough pain; you might as well get on back to Ohio."

Together Tom and Carl descended the stairs. "Mister Hall, I'll have one of my deputies take you to the hotel; it's too damn cold to be walking tonight."

Alone now, with his feet on his desk Carl cradled a hot coffee in his lap and tipped his chair almost to the point of overturning. *Son of a bitch,* Carl thought as he sat alone in his office once more. *That young Hall looks like he might cause some trouble. Just when I've got things under control and going my way leave it to some do-gooder to butt his nose in.*

CHAPTER NINE

Every fiber of Warren's body felt like it was afire. As he lay on the hard jail bunk now he tried to understand what was happening to him.

In just two weeks his life had gone from something wonderful, with a decent job and a wonderful girlfriend, to an absolute nightmare. Never in his wildest dreams could he have imagined he would end up lying here in the county jail. The worst was that the sheriff sounded absolutely convinced that there was ample evidence to send him to jail for killing Timmy Coyle….for a murder he didn't commit! Compared to that, the manslaughter charge for running over that laborer seemed like the least of his worries. That was something else Warren couldn't figure out.

"What in the world happened to Timmy?" Warren knew Timmy was a hot-head braggart, spoiled and used to having everything his own way. He had the clothes, the car, the endless supply of money, and the gaggle of goons who followed him like the rats after the pied piper. Timmy just expected everything to be his way and at his choosing, and Warren just tried to stay out of his way whenever possible. "Maybe if I hadn't gone to the dance, really stayed out of his way, this all might not have happened."

But of course Warren hadn't stayed away from the dances. Like most young men living in Chippewa County, Warren liked going to the dances. It was usually just an enjoyable time, and the dance was a good place to meet his friends on a Saturday night. If not for the hard-times dances Warren guessed the only entertainment in the whole county was throwing horseshoes, and it was pretty hard to do that in the middle of winter.

The hard-times dances had begun in Montevideo, as in other rural communities, during the depression years. The dances were just inexpensive entertainment, a placed to get together with friends for a fun time. No one expected to get all dressed up. As a matter of fact, during the depression, many of the folks around Monte had little option regarding dressing up. They were too poor to spend money on fancy clothes, so settled for being clean and having a fun time.

The depression tradition of hard-times dances had continued, even as the economy improved and although prohibition had ended, Chippewa County was still a "dry" county and those who wanted to drink brought their own liquor. Most of the people were drinking moonshine these days, brought up from Iowa, and they bought set-ups at the dance. The liquor could be mixed with Coke, or Squirt, or Seven-up, but mostly the men nipped at the bottle which they kept in a pocket or just sitting on the table in open defiance of a foolish and outdated law.

On some Saturdays there would be dancing at the Sons of Norway Hall in Montevideo, but most often if the guys were going to meet in Monte, the Eagles Club downtown, or at the National Guard Armory up near Windom College was the place to be on Saturday night. That, Warren recalled, was where he and Timmy had their first meeting.

On a typical Saturday however, there were several other gathering spots round the county, and Buster's Roadhouse was one of Warren's favorites. One of the advantages of Buster's for Warren was that Timmy and his gang of goons didn't always show up there, although that couldn't always be counted on. If Warren had thought of Timmy at all that Saturday in January, he must have thought it unlikely Timmy would brave the stormy night to find his way to Buster's.

"Jesus," Warren thought as he tried to find a position on the bunk that didn't aggravate the stabbing pain in his chest, "how could I end up in so much trouble without the slightest idea how it all happened?" Fighting the pain in his chest that jabbed and jabbed at him Warren felt the room spin, floating as he tried to recall when his world began to change.

CHAPTER
TEN
January 29, 1938

Warren's Dodge coupe purred along, the high tires pushing snow in wide wakes from either side of the car. The large headlights cut silver channels through the early evening and the blowing snow. Warren hummed a nameless tune as he sped along, smiling as he thought of the evening ahead.

It had been snowing all day in Montevideo. If not for the snow, the world around Warren might have shimmered, under a huge canopy of winter stars and the North Star would have been overhead but tonight Warren's world was blanketed in an undulating cotton candy of swirling snow. As he drove from town the snow foamed and swirled like a huge river that engulfed the entire countryside as the huge flakes of snow nestled one with the other. "It's hard to believe each flake can possibly be different from all the others." It was beyond Warren's comprehension.

Well, snow or not, Saturday had been a workday at Swift's, but now that day was over and it was time to unwind. He was on his way to pick up Jeanne and head out to Buster's.

In Minneapolis, WCCO radio announcers were cautioning that dangerous conditions were settling over the prairies, thrusting cold white fingers into the river forests, while WNAX in Yankton, South Dakota, had gone beyond those mild warnings, and was now announcing that extreme cold and wind would combine to envelope South Dakota and the adjoining states in the most severe blizzard of the winter.

Even though the residents of the Minnesota River Valley were being warned of the imminent storm closing in on them, life continued nearly normal in Montevideo and the surrounding countryside. It wasn't that folks here were unaware of winter's dangers, but they accepted the storms as part of life. Warren was no different than the others, and tonight he and Jeanne would go to Buster's Roadhouse for a night of dancing, drinking, and socializing with their friends.

Buster's little roadside bait and lunch business had grown to roadhouse capacity, with dances every Saturday. It kept Buster busy seven days a week just as working at Swift and Company in Montevideo kept Warren employed.

Warren and Buster had grown up together in Kragero Township. They were two country boys, and proud to be so. They had been together since the beginning of school, inseparable friends who shared uncounted boyhood experiences.

On Saturday nights the two still found time to be close pals. The only difference these days was the presence of Jeanne. Last year she had popped back into Warren's life.

Warren had been playing horseshoes one evening early last summer in Watson, playing well, too. That is, he played well until Jeanne showed up. When he first saw Jeanne he didn't recognize her as the same pug nosed girl with pigtails who had grown up on another farm just a few miles down the road from Warren. It was an altogether different girl, a young woman really, who stood at the corner of the café next to the horseshoe yard watching him, than the girl he last remembered seeing.

Jeanne and her friend Dolly watched as Warren's usually perfect game fell apart. Dolly talked almost nonstop as the two girls watched. The talking didn't bother Warren at all, but Jeanne's stare soon drove him to distraction. He wondered for a moment if she knew that she was staring at him.

Jeanne was tiny, not an inch over five feet tall he was sure, and her eyes, were large and trusting, soft brown and they sparkled in the bright overhead lights. Framed as they were by her short auburn hair they somehow made him think of a gentle lamb. Warren's eyes drifted toward her as he lined up for his next toss, two big brown eyes that twinkled with mischief as they looked at him. He missed his toss.

Jeanne wore a sparkling white blouse and the way it tucked into her form fitting skirt accented the swell of her breasts and hips against her tiny waist. "Where did SHE come from? Concentrate," Warren told himself. As he strode forward to release the next heavy steel shoe he stared hard at the iron shaft rising from the dirt, planting his right foot firmly as his left hand swung the horseshoe through its arc. Then, as he released the shoe his eye flickered at a slight movement. Jeanne, turning to respond to Dolly's last comment, was outlined against the night, the flood light above the horseshoe pits shone on her like a stage light.

"Oh Christ, Warren!" His horseshoe partner exploded, "where did that come from?" Warren's last, last toss of the night, sent the horseshoe caroming past the steel post and across the yard, flopping finally like a grounded fish in the grass at the edge of the yard, and

Warren stormed away with his hands thrown up in disgust as his opponents and usual well-wishers laughed at his grand exit.

Now, a year later, Jeanne was the center of Warren's life just as the bar was the center of Buster's life. The difference of course was that Jeanne was soft and warm. Warren and Buster shared a buddies' love, but what Warren and Jeanne shared was something Warren had never known existed and was a love that had brought new meaning and excitement to his life. With the week's work complete now Warren was anxious to reach Jeanne.

Just as Warren felt especially lucky to have Jeanne, he also felt lucky to be working at Swift's. Swift and Company was a big outfit handling poultry and dairy products, and Warren drove truck for them six days a week. The company had a big plant in Smith's Addition, out on the west edge of Montevideo, where in large concrete and tile rooms the employees processed, packed, and shipped farm products. Six days a week Warren and the other drivers brought in chickens, ducks, and turkeys, as well as eggs and milk, which was turned into good rich butter, that Warren thought was almost as good as his ma made on the farm. Each of the drivers had established routes, traveling to smaller community creameries throughout the Minnesota River Valley, which served as a form of relay stations between the farms and Swift and Company.

On Saturdays, the crew mostly wrapped up all the unfinished business of the week and gave the plant an extra cleanup. Warren, however, made one more trip in his truck. Saturday was a short run to the creamery in Dawson to pick up milk, then to Boyd for the last pick up of the week which was usually a half dozen cases of eggs and as many cans of milk.

Most times of the year the steel milk cans, which Warren stacked two high by the time his Saturday trip was complete, were clanging deafeningly in the back of the truck as Warren sped along the graveled roads. Today, however, the roads were covered with the fresh snow which had been falling about him all day, and the trip back to Monte had been quiet, if somewhat stormy.

When he returned to the plant, Warren backed against the cement loading dock at the end of the building and swung the long roller-conveyor onto the truck so he could begin unloading his cargo. Despite the cold he worked in his shirt sleeves, yanking each can to the back of the truck and sliding it onto the steel rollers, where it tracked slowly into the plant. The shiny guards on the conveyor, polished daily by the passing steel cans, kept those cans from crashing onto the loading dock, and as they rattled across the rollers the sound reminded Warren of the train wheels passing over steel rails. By the time the cans were all unloaded Warren felt a pleasant glow but had not really worked up a sweat.

Leaving the truck backed up to the dock he shuffled through the snow into the cool plant which was now vacant except for the watchman who was wandering someplace in the building complex. On Saturday it was also Warren's job to stack the milk cans and egg crates from his load into one of the huge coolers where the milk and eggs would remain chilled until the Monday morning shift began, and to receipt each creamery's shipment. By Monday night, all this milk would be well on its way to becoming butter but now it needed to be stacked in the cooler.

Warren put eight cans to a cart load. Nine cart loads today, loaded, hauled, unloaded onto the cart, and then hauled to the cooler, where they were handled once more. Even being raised with the rigorous life on the farm, at first Warren found the routine of being a driver at Swift's demanding work. But after a few weeks on the truck he'd gotten used to shoving and lifting the one hundred-twenty odd pound cans of milk. Now he could do it hours on end when called upon to do so. He actually enjoyed the exertion; "good clean work," he thought.

As a result of the daily routine his five foot eleven inch frame was lean and powerful, although at a hundred sixty five pounds he looked to some casual observers like nothing more than a displaced farm kid. It was that kind of mistake in judgment which had gotten Timmy Coyle into trouble at the hard-times dance a couple of weeks earlier.

CHAPTER
ELEVEN

January 29, 1938

Although the wind kicked the hard snow tightly against their house, Timmy Coyle and his parents were hardly aware of the storm's increasing intensity. Their large Victorian home, tucked inside its own comfortable park was well-built and well protected from the weather by the giant evergreens landscaped among a dozen ancient oaks and elms. From its comfortable vantage at the crest of the Second Street hill, the Coyle's had watched rain and snow, tornadoes, dust storms and beautiful sunsets across the wide valley below them. Nothing ever touched them in their safe retreat.

Just visible in the trees below their house, was a channel of the Chippewa River, with a wide lagoon, which had been created when a concrete dam had been built to control some of the river's infamous flooding.

In the summer Timmy's mother loved to watch the young people from her high vantage point, canoeing or rowing their tiny boats in the lagoon. She thought it was romantic, the girls with their parasols sitting in the back of the boat while the young men toured them around the lagoon. Sometimes she would see a boat bobbing idly in the lily pads, the couple embracing as if unaware of the rest of the world. Sometimes as she watched the young people Emma felt herself floating also. It was as if she floated right out of her body, out of the big quiet house.

Now, as Emma gazed out at the swirling snow she could hear soft music playing, coming from some place she was not quite able to locate. Soft strains of a Strauss waltz sifted through the dusk and she felt as if she were dancing, floating across the lush green lawn in a park of giant oak trees. How handsome Herman was, so tall and strong as he gently guided her. . . two, three, four, one, two. . . over and over, turning and gliding, spinning endlessly, they were like angels floating among the clouds. Emma's long white gown whispered softly around her as the two lovers glided among the trees. Although she couldn't remember exactly why, Emma felt this was the most wonderful day of her life, the day for which she had lived.

As they danced, she felt Herman's strong hand pressed knowingly against her, plying her delicate skin through the fragile material as his eyes gazed upon the ample swell of her breasts which threatened to push their way free of the gown's low cut bodice.

Emma blushed slightly as she thought of Herman's hard beautiful body, the way they fit together so perfectly. On and on she danced as if the rest of the world ceased to exist, the beautiful music carrying her as if in a dream.

The entire valley below the Coyle's house was a park. The Minnesota and Chippewa Rivers joined further downstream, but just below Emma's window the Chippewa River formed a beautiful lagoon where the water shimmered so wonderfully. All around the lagoon were huge oak trees where one could walk for hours and escape the depressing world.

Some of the townspeople, her own husband included, complained that their taxes had gone up too much because of all the work needed to maintain such a large park. But to Emma the park had become a perfect escape, her only escape, from the boredom and discontent she found in her marriage.

Everyone at the country club thought she had such a wonderful life, her husband being such a successful businessman and all. And she saw the envy in the eyes of the women, even strangers as she and Herman would promenade to the Riverside Hotel for dinner, or just pass along Main Street in Herman's new Cadillac. What they didn't know of course was what a tyrant Herman really was and what a spoiled brat their only son had become. She guessed, however, that by now people might have seen how spoiled Timmy was.

Somehow Emma's relationship with her husband had changed after Timmy was born. Before then she remembered that Herman had been kind and affectionate, and he had treated her with respect. Even in the initial stages of her pregnancy he had taken her to bed frequently, made love to her with wild passion. "God'" she thought, "How I miss that, even after all these years." But something had changed over the years. Now he growled and snapped at her like he was a mad dog chained up in a junk yard. What made it even worse was now Timmy had begun to treat her the same way, as if she were the hired help. She hardly dared think her lovely son might be responsible for her sadness. "No. It must be something else; certainly not Timmy."

Herman had doted on their only son from the day he was born. There was never anything Timmy asked for that his dad hadn't provided. It was fortunate the Men's Store was so successful, providing not only their very acceptable social standing, but also providing more and more expensive toys needed to keep their son happy.

Herman and Timmy rarely had discordant words, mostly because what Timmy wanted Herman was only too happy to give. Tonight, however, was one of those bad times between them. Even in the raging storm Timmy insisted he was going out. "I'm just going up to Watson, for God's sake!"

"I don't think it's a good idea, son," Herman placated. "Look how the snow's gotten heavier just in the last hour."

Every argument posed by his father brought another angry response. "Dad, I was brought up in weather like this. Don't you think I can drive, for Christ's sake?' In fact Timmy had been driving for more than ten years. In the beginning Herman had bored the men at the country club night after night with stories of Timmy's wonderful handling of the car as, under Herman's direction, they sped across the county. "Oh, yes," Herman bragged, "Timmy's reflexes were so unusual for a fifteen year old boy." Later, when alone, Timmy's driving had turned to recklessness. None of Herman's friends dared confront Herman about his spoiled son's driving. Nor did they dare discuss Timmy's other unpleasant habits, except among themselves, when Herman was elsewhere.

"Besides, Dad, if I take your Caddie, it's heavy enough to plow through anything! C'mon now, you know I'll be all right. Besides, I'm supposed to pick up a couple of the guys. They're expecting me."

After much shouting and cajoling Timmy won another battle with his father. After all, he had more than a quarter of a century of experience, had learned long ago how to wear down his father's will. "If you're going to treat me like a child," the final threat, "….I'll just move out. Is that what you want?"

As the two men in her life prowled through the house arguing about the storm Emma listened to the waltz playing so soothingly in her mind. From the big bay window she watched the snow swirling across the hillsides, filling the world with gentle, soft white snow, hiding her and her beloved Herman in its gauzy softness As they danced across the lazy lagoon and through the park, they smiled lovingly into each other's eyes.

CHAPTER

TWELVE

Sometimes, when she allowed herself to think about it Timmy worried Emma. Some of Timmy's friends were not the kind of young men she thought he should spent too much time with. She knew some of them were the kind who could lead Timmy astray, the kind whose parents lived on the other side of town out on State Highway or in Smith's Addition. She had seen the kind of people they were and had heard Herman at the Country Club as he described how awful they were. They were the kind who worked at that awful Swift's plant, killing chickens and who knew what all, or were the sweaty, dirty men who did construction work, and used awful language.

Even Carl Brown, the new sheriff who had come to Montevideo from Granite Falls last year seemed to be one of Timmy's friends. She shuddered when she remembered how he looked at her, as though he could see right through her clothes and was putting his filthy hands all over her. One day Timmy had even told Emma he might get a job as a deputy, that he thought the sheriff was quite a guy. Emma felt uneasy when Timmy talked like that. She couldn't understand why her son didn't just go to work at the Men's Store like Herman. After all, look how much good it had done for her and Herman. Timmy was working for the railroad now, but said he was going to get away from there as soon as something good came along.

As far as Timmy was concerned railroading was just too damn much work for someone like him. He knew he was cut out for better things and he knew for sure he wasn't going to work in that damn clothing store and waste his entire life like his father had done, selling shoes and all that crap to just anybody who walked in the door.

He had graduated from the high school in Montevideo. Then he had put in two trouble filled years at Windom College before they bounced him out the winter of his second year. Even all the clout Timmy's old man had at the school didn't help that time, Timmy angrily remembered. Hung over as hell, Timmy had pushed another student off the side of the ski jump at the college one morning and busted the kid up pretty badly. "The dumb bastard deserved it," Timmy had barked at his companions later on. The college had installed the ski jump just the year before, along with the new toboggan run a little nearer the huge brick educational building. Timmy and a half dozen other students enrolled in winter athletic courses had finally qualified to use the jump. Although he hadn't let on to anyone, Timmy was scared as hell the first time he climbed the tower to the ski jump. Once up, however, there was no way he would lose face by not jumping.

The rush Timmy felt as he left the ramp that first time was indescribable; floating above the long slope he could see the entire valley as he drifted back to earth. It gave Timmy a feeling of power and dominance; he wanted to float there forever.

Over the next several days Timmy polished his skill, knowing he would become Montevideo's first ski jumper to win an inter-school competition when the upcoming invitational was held at the college. One thing bothered him, however. There was a rumor the coach might pick Dan Severson instead of Timmy to jump for Monte. In spite of every effort Timmy had made to outdistance them, Dan and his bean pole pal Dickie Canton had nearly matched him jump for jump the past two days.

On Monday morning, just four days before the meet, Timmy had shown up in a particularly foul mood left over from a weekend of intense partying and drinking. After blowing his first jump he found himself behind Dan on the ladderway up the ski jump. He hadn't really pushed Dan off the jump as some observers claimed, but while rousting Dan, trying to shake his confidence, Timmy had grabbed Dan's skis and gave them a hard yank. At the same time, he thought it would be funny to jab his own skis into Dan's crotch."

What Timmy hadn't counted on, however, was Dan slipping on a patch of ice as he turned to confront Timmy. Timmy's jerk on the skis unbalanced Dan and the combination of the ice and the skis twisted tight into his groin sent Dan flailing into the handrail, then as the others watched in horror he slipped beneath the rail and bounced several times against the framing timbers as he fell twenty feet to the hard ground.

Dan Severson was soon ambulanced to the hospital, to spend several weeks recovering from a broken collarbone, some broken ribs, and a broken arm as well as a badly bruised face. Although Timmy swore it was an accident, there were enough witnesses who were tired of Timmy's bullying and who knew of the recent bad blood between the two students to prove otherwise.

This was just another case of Timmy wanting to have his own way and getting it without any concern for others. The difference was that this time none of

Timmy's cronies were around to alibi for him, and the first thing Timmy knew, he'd been bounced right out of school, and into the real world, while Dickie Canton skied to Windom College's first interschool record.

CHAPTER

THIRTEEN

For Timmy, growing up in Montevideo had been like having a permanent birthday party. Herman provided everything a son could ask for, and Timmy learned very early to keep asking. From his first tricycle, which was the best around, to his first car, and his second and then his third, Timmy had learned to have his way. Good clothes, new car, always money in his pocket when others were broke; these were the things that were important and having them brought Timmy power.

What Timmy wanted; Timmy got. His father had shown time and again that the Coyles were a step above everyone else. They were several steps above the farmers, however. He had learned well from his father; damn farmers were just a pain in the ass and second class at best.

For one thing, the young men from town, like Timmy, were better educated,. Most of those who grew up in town graduated from the twelfth grade now, and were making more money, thanks to the railroad. Sometimes they liked to lord it over the farm boys, and that too seemed natural to Herman.

Employment had been scarce around Montevideo since the beginning of the depression, but things had started looking up recently. The railroad was hiring men and the new flood control project out by Watson was going to keep a lot of men employed for a while yet. Some of the boys who didn't work for the railroad like

Timmy, were able to work on WPA projects around the area, and even at forty-four dollars a month, these boys from Monte earned a lot more money than the young farmers. A few of Timmy's friends also drove shiny cars; not as shiny as Timmy's of course, and they all wore fashionable clothes. To Herman, clothes made the man. And Timmy learned from Herman of course.

Most of the lessons Timmy learned from his father were put to immediate use. One of the easiest lessons for Timmy to practice was keeping the farmers in their place. That was usually pretty easy. It seemed that all the farmers Timmy met were just willing to be pushed around. They'd just turn and walk quietly away, slinking back to their old smelly cars. Some of them even came to town in pickup trucks! Timmy didn't have to lean on them very hard to have his way. "Maybe," he jeered, "they're all retarded from smelling all that cow shit!" All his friends laughed at that joke.

Timmy had disliked Warren from their first meeting. A *REAL* farmer, Timmy could tell right away. As a matter of fact, Timmy's old man, who owned the best men's store in Montevideo, didn't even like Warren's old man. "Smelly goddamn farmers!" That was all old man Coyle needed to know about them.

It was Timmy's style to strut and bluster, just like his father, intimidating anyone he thought he could intimidate and showing his big toothy political smile to those he wanted to brown nose. Warren was not on the list Timmy wanted to cultivate, however. It stood to reason, therefore, that Warren must be on the list and needed to be intimidated.

It came as a sudden surprise to Timmy that Warren was not much impressed with Timmy's bullying style. Their first meeting hadn't gone as Timmy planned. Timmy had arrived with a flourish at one of the hard-time dances at the Armory trailed by a gaggle of his hang-abouts, and Timmy prepared to establish the ground rules for the tall lanky farmer. With his friends egging him on Timmy had confronted the newcomer. Establishing his dominance early was very important to Timmy since he knew any failure to maintain his posture would undermine his popularity and his leadership.

Making noises about cow-shit smelling farmers who belonged in the barn, Timmy began pushing Warren, ordering him out of the dance. From time to time he threw out stage whispers to his crowd "....ever see shit stacked this high?" That brought lots of laughs from the boys.

At first it seemed that Warren was going to leave without a hassle. The farmers usually did, Timmy knew. Push by push, from the main floor of the Armory toward the entry Timmy pursued him and backing down the half-flight of stairs Warren retreated under the mostly verbal barrage. Then came the surprise.

There was hardly time for Timmy to react to the change in the young farm boy's attitude. After about two more pushes and three cow-shit farmer comments Warren decided he had been pushed far enough. In the several minutes it took for the battlefield to shift to the relative quiet of the entryway, Warren hadn't spoken, hadn't offered resistance to Timmy's advancing army. Then, moving back and sideways a half step Warren had suddenly responded in a manner Timmy wasn't at all used to.

With a short spring loaded right that started at his own waist Warren explained to Timmy and to all those present the difference between them. He simply cold cocked young Timmy Coyle. With a single blow, without saying a word, he had challenged Timmy's dominance as it had never been challenged and had rewritten the rules of conduct to include a new chapter on how not to deal with Warren Marshall.

In addition to splitting Timmy's lip, Warren's single knock-out blow had broken Timmy's nose and the power behind the blow caused Timmy's eyes to blacken and swell shut almost immediately. It would take a month for the damage to Timmy's face to heal, and even then, Timmy's nose remained slightly, but permanently, left of center. The damage to Timmy's ego would take much longer to be repaired.

Without a second look Warren returned to the dance floor, leaving out like a proverbial light, his entourage of also-rans standing in awe.

CHAPTER
FOURTEEN
February 17, 1938

Tom Hall sat picking at his breakfast. The dining room of the Riverside Hotel was sunny and bright now as the morning sun reflected against the snow covered street. Unlike when he arrived last night, this morning was calm, but still cold. The snow which had filled the air last night now settled again on the street outside the hotel window. An air of melancholy held Tom this morning and he felt lethargic as he thought about his arrival here the preceding evening.

The stationmaster had spoken the truth when he told Tom it would be a long cold walk to the courthouse. Once he arrived at the jail Tom found himself thrown into a disconcerting world he was just now trying to analyze.

When he entered the courthouse and found his way to the sheriff's office, Tom had every intention of hating the man who had killed his brother, but he was not prepared to see the slender young man who had been beaten so horribly by the sheriff. The fear and anguish Tom saw in Warren's eyes had shaken Tom's resolve. His instincts told him the man in the cell did not have the look of a killer, a devious man, a man with no conscience who could knowingly leave another to die beside the road.

"You've got to believe me, Mister..." As Tom thought again of Warren's pain filled plea he began to think there might be more to this story than he had so far learned.

As he was wiping a drop of coffee from his lower lip a shadow crossed between Tom and the dining room's large windows. Looking up, Tom saw a pale young woman who had stopped and now stood shyly at his table. She was very tiny. Before his eyes focused and he actually looked at her, Tom had expected to see her parents pull the child away, scolding her for staring at the stranger. But as he placed his napkin on the table Tom realized the large brown eyes staring at him belonged to a very beautiful tiny young woman.

Tom flashed the young woman his best Washington, D.C. smile. "Well good morning. And how can I help you?" He was drawn to her large brown eyes, staring so intently back at him, and in spite of the bundle of winter clothing she wore, Tom recognized her beauty.

"Are you Mister Hall?" the young woman asked as she timidly looked into Tom's eyes.

"Why, yes, I am. Would you care to join me?" Tom responded, half rising and motioning to the chair across from him. He hadn't the slightest idea who this lovely young creature was or where this conversation would lead, but it was not in his manner to ignore the many possibilities such a meeting offered.

Without speaking the young woman swept the wrinkles from her coat and skirt as she sat, and Tom watched silently, still taken by her extraordinary beauty. He thought if this girl were in Washington she would be lost. Her beauty is so natural and unpremeditated, not like the girls from the big city who would rely on chic clothes and flashy makeup to define their beauty.

Tom's experience in Washington, D.C. had been extensive. For three years his Navy assignments had thrown him into almost daily contact with the fast life of an international city. The best of the beautiful were all around him. Almost without exception they left him cold. It wasn't that Tom disliked women, but that when these young girls left their homes and families behind them they seemed to go through a metamorphosis. It seemed to Tom that every woman who came to Washington, D.C. had graduated from the same correspondence school, dressing, speaking, and eating in exactly the same prescribed manner. They wore the same smiles painted on porcelain faces, rouged, and mascaraed, they smiled vaguely while they babbled inanely beyond their level of intelligence.

In all those months Tom had only once found a relationship that had meant anything to him. Unfortunately for him, at that same time, Uncle Sam had played a cruel trick by sending him to England on a mission. When he returned the lady of his dreams had disappeared.

"Now," Tom looked deeply into her brown eyes, seeing anguish there for the first time, "tell me who you are, and what brings such a lovely creature like you after me on a morning like this."

With her back erect Jeanne stared at Tom for a long moment then began. "Mister Hall, my name is Jeanne Amundson. Warren…." she paused. "I was with him the night he was supposed to have run over your brother. I just had to talk to you." She was on the verge of tears. "I just had to talk to someone."

Mister Hall," she continued, "I know you've come to make arrangements to take your brother home. The whole town already knows you went to the jail last night to see Warren. And I know the sheriff has told you how bad Warren is, how perhaps he even ran over you're your brother on purpose, and how he beat Timmy Coyle to death in the alley. But...you have to believe me; we did not kill your brother. Oh, it's possible he was lying in the snow just as the sheriff says. We had an awful blizzard that weekend. The snow was as deep as my waist before it was over." In fact, before the storm ended, Chippewa County farmers recorded drifts up to twelve feet high and for days after the storm the only travel was on foot or horse drawn sleigh. "Warren and I were dancing at Buster's. Like most everyone there, we were drinking, too. Perhaps Warren was even a little drunk, but I know Warren didn't kill your brother as the sheriff has said."

Jeanne wrung her hands nervously, "And when Timmy Coyle was killed, that Saturday night after Warren was let out of jail, well, Warren and I were not even in Montevideo."

Without pausing to let Tom get a word in she continued, as if she had to get everything said while she still had the nerve to speak out. "You see, Timmy had cornered Warren earlier in the evening as we were planning to go to a movie at the new Monte Theatre. I don't know why Timmy is...was...always trying to pick a fight with Warren. It's just like he couldn't stand the idea of us being together or something. He was such a bully. But after that confrontation we decided we weren't in any mood to see a movie so we got in Warren's car and drove down to Wegdahl. We do that sometimes; we like to drive around sometimes and..." She blushed momentarily, "and, well, we just talk. We didn't get home until very late that night. When we came back we passed right outside of Monte on highway fifty-nine. That highway doesn't even go through town. We didn't come through town. There's no way Warren could have been here in Montevideo at the time Timmy was murdered."

By now tears were streaming down Jeanne's cheeks. Her back was no longer stiff and straight; instead, she hunched forward, seeming all the tinier in her anguish.

"Miss...Jeanne." Tom stammered. "Collect yourself for a moment. This is all coming just a little too fast for me. I'm not sure just what's going on here." Logic was telling Tom that the sheriff must be right. How could he make judgments regarding Warren's guilt or innocence based only on walking in and seeing Warren for just a few minutes? Granted, Warren had been beaten up, but as the sheriff said, Warren had tried to fight them off, so maybe the sheriff and his deputies had just been overzealous in performing their duties.

How could he know from just a dozen quickly spoken words whether the man was guilty or innocent of the crimes he was accused of committing? The young woman across from him here brought out the romantic in Tom, brought out the protective fatherly instinct which surprised him. He was almost willing himself to succumb to her cries of innocence. After all, Warren was now in the jail for a second death. Whom should he believe? *Or, Tom mused, should he even worry about it at all.*

"I must say however, I've got some questions of my own, based on what the sheriff told me and what I saw in the jail last night. Maybe you'd be kind enough, when you've had a moment, to tell me just what this is all about. Tell me what's happened. If, as you say, Warren isn't responsible for my brother's death or for the death of that other young man, Jeanne, then tell me why the sheriff is so intent on having the blame placed on him."

As Jeanne sought to control herself she sat straighter in the chair and wiped the tears from her cheeks. Tom motioned the waitress to bring more coffee and a fresh cup for Jeanne. Silently she placed the cup in front of Jeanne and poured the hot black coffee. With this task completed she looked down her long straight nose as if she had already judged not only Warren, but Jeanne also. With a quiet "Humph" she turned and left them staring at her trail.

"Now, Jeanne, please call me Tom; and please, tell me as much as you can about how this whole mess has come about. I'm not sure I really understand what's happened here."

"Boy, isn't that the understatement of the year!" Tom thought. "The only thing I am sure of is that when I arrived home I found my mother crying quietly in her chair and on the table next to her was a telegram explaining my brother was dead and that his killer was in jail."

"The only thing I know," he continued to Jeanne, "is that I'm in The Middle of Nowhere, Minnesota…with the weather cold as heck," he chuckled. "The man who's supposed to have killed my brother is in jail charged with the death of another man as well, and the sheriff is doing everything he can to convince me what a bad fellow Warren is. What I can't seem to get straight in my mind is why, with all the supposed evidence, Warren doesn't seem as guilty to me as he should. I'm not even sure why I want to listen to another side of this grizzly business. I should just claim my brother's body and get back on the train."

But there was something going on here, something about the conflicting stories that Tom needed to figure out. His experience in Washington, D.C., and other places he didn't talk about had taught him to trust his instincts. "If something smelled rotten," he had learned, "it was probably rotten." So, as Jeanne described the events of the preceding weeks Tom sipped his coffee, trying hard not to think of how beautiful she was, and taking notes of the questions he now wanted answered.

Chapter
Fifteen
February 6, 1938

Carl could tell it was going to be one of those days; one of those days that followed one of those nights with too much to drink and the frustration he felt all too frequently in recent days. This morning before the cobwebs had begun to clear from his head Jeanne's image had flashed into his mind. Before he remembered he was alone in his dingy room, Carl's mind told him he could feel her long smooth legs around him, taste her salty perspiration as he kissed her breasts while he snuggled against them. Carl was filled with a mixture of anger and hollow disappointment as she re-materialized into his pillow, the sweat coming from his own face as he opened his eyes, alone in his stale bed.

Carl could not get Jeanne out of his mind; all day it went on and on. It was as if the more he tried not to think about Jeanne the more he did think about her. Although it was Sunday, his official day off, he went to the jail, threw himself into the stack of paperwork that had called for his attention for weeks. Occasionally, when he thought of her being with Warren, it made Carl's blood boil, angry that he was forced to share her.

All the while he had been following the county snowplow to the Amundson's farm last Sunday Carl had been distracted by thoughts of Jeanne. When he failed to respond to his deputies' questions that morning they attributed his slow response to a lack of sleep. But Carl, even though sorely needing sleep, had been thinking of Jeanne. The rhythm of the Ford patrol car's windshield wipers sweeping away the raging snow became the pounding tempo of the small country band, and in the haze Carl saw Jeanne's long pale legs disappearing into the shadows of her skirt; from the shadows of those long soft legs there came a whisper, an echo calling him, "Carl...Carl...Carl." It whispered to him like the wind seeping through the car's door.

He was sure Jeanne hadn't been wearing any underwear last night, that he had seen her soft thatch of downy hair beckoning him. As he had crossed the room his temperature rose at her rich sweaty womaness. He was surprised no one else had responded. But that only proved the animal in her had been calling just to him, calling for him to enter her, to treat her as a woman wanted to be treated, needed to be treated.

Step by step, Carl had crossed the room. In his mind he was already feeling himself thrusting deep inside her, slamming hard against her pelvis as she writhed beneath him, her legs abandoned to the air as she screamed *More, faster, harder, damn it! Fuck me like it's the end of the world you wonderful son of a bitch!* Then, in the space of a half dozen steps, she was gone, cloistered in a booth with that son-of-a-bitch Warren and his friends and Carl was forced back to the reality of the moment, but her willing image was still with him.

During the past week Carl had seen Jeanne two or three times, when she came to visit Warren, before he was released from jail on bail, and again when Carl had been investigating the crime. Carl was unwilling to even consider it less than manslaughter.

Jeanne had appeared cool, reserved, when she saw Carl, but he was sure it was only a façade. Carl knew how irresistible he was to women. Some women just played a little hard to get. Of course he could understand how Jeanne wouldn't want to show her interest when Warren was with her, but once alone Carl knew that was going to change, that she was going to be pliable as putty in his hands. "She doesn't know what she's missing yet, but that will change."

Every woman in a tight skirt caught Carl's attention. Even the homeliest woman was worth the time it took Carl to mentally undress, especially if she had a good looking ass. "Anybody who's not an ass man doesn't know where it's at," Carl chuckled. Tall or short, it didn't matter to Carl, and if she had long legs that was all the better in Carl's judgment. At the end, however, they all made him think of Jeanne. She was his dream woman, his dream woman, and his fantasy of fantasies. All day Carl's thoughts came back to Jeanne, and in his fantasies he found the satisfaction he never found in his own life.

By the time the sun had set Carl was sexually charged and needed desperately to find someone to throw his switch. He locked his desk and left the courthouse, a man with a frantic if unrecognized need. All thoughts but sex had now been driven from his head.

In his small room at the boarding house near the depot Carl had showered and shaved, slapping on big hands full of aftershave. He again judged himself superior to any other man as he gazed at his reflection in the cloudy mirror. Gut sucked in and his shoulders thrown back, Carl knew what a catch he was for any woman astute enough to try to catch him. He slicked his hair back a final time; then out the door he went.

The sheriff's Ford was heading south. *Maybe I'll stop in Clarkfield,* Carl thought. *Or maybe I should stop in Boyd first, see what was going on there.* Wherever he ended up, there would only be one thing on Carl's mind tonight; he wouldn't be satisfied until he had gotten laid.

As he swung south on Main Street, crossing the railroad tracks as he left town he reached under the seat for the bottle nestled there. With one hand he loosened the top, dropping it on the seat. The paper bag whispered against his cheek as he hoisted the bottle for a couple of quick belts while he guided the Ford out of town.

On a Sunday night the little beer joint in Clarkfield usually contained a mixture of customers. Even in the winter people had to get out once in a while, get away from the kids or the wife, for a couple of hours before facing the world again on Monday.

As he entered the tavern Carl's eyes swept the room. At a corner table, separated from the mostly white crowd, three swarthy men sat somberly sipping their beers. They glared from under furrowed brows at the one unwelcome man in their midst. Perched on one of the tall chrome stools with red leatherette covers was Carl Brown. Next to him sat a young woman known to the three somber men at the table, a woman who, like them, lived at the Agency. Tonight Carl was not here in the capacity of Chippewa County sheriff, but just a middle aged man looking for a quick and easy piece from one of the Indian girls whom he favored.

Nonetheless, everyone in the tavern knew Carl, and they knew his reputation. They knew Carl too well, and no one here would dare to stand against him. He was big and mean with a reputation for being cruel and vicious. Some thought him a little crazy.

On a night not unlike this two years ago another girl had found herself in this position, and when another man had gotten in Carl's way, daring to confront him in a tavern in Granite Falls, the friend ended up losing his life without ever understanding why.

The young girl sitting next to Carl this night was becoming uncomfortable under the cold stares of the men at the corner table. She flinched as Carl, whose mood had not mellowed through several hours of drinking occasionally pawed at her, and she averted her eyes as much as possible when he stared at her face or tracked his eyes down the front of her blouse.

When she had first joined him much earlier this evening his mood had been more pleasant, but now he was getting surly and obnoxious; there seemed to be no way to get away from his grasp. Somehow she found his gaze hypnotic, like a snake which has a mouse almost cornered. Although the mouse could escape if it leaped and ran, for some reason it had to stay, to see what the snake was going to do next. In the end, the mouse would be devoured, and the snake, with a satiated smile, would wind its way home to sleep.

CHAPTER

SIXTEEN
February 19, 1938

Jeanne sat stiffly on the edge of her bed. Her mind was racing and her thoughts were uncontrolled and without direction. For the past year, her life had been a wonderful dream. Her waking thoughts had been only of Warren and how happy she was when he was near. Throughout the weeks as she did her chores, helped her ma in the house, she thought only of the preceding weekends and of the coming Saturdays when she would again be with Warren. How glorious it is to be in love! She laughed each time she thought it.

Now, here she sat, utterly devastated by the events of the last two weeks. There had been no sense that anything was amiss as she and Warren had braved the storm as they slowly challenged the drifting snow between Buster's and her parents' farm. It hadn't taken long for Warren to sober up and begin concentrating on his driving as the swept through the stormy night. At times, the snow blew so violently that even the front of Warren's Dodge was hidden from sight. There were several times, when driving slowly in second gear, they feared they would not be able to plow the car through one more snowdrift.

Several times when the wind slacked for a moment Warren found he had lost his direction, that the car was nearly off the road, and with a sudden wrench of the steering wheel he fought the car back to the temporary safety of the roadway hidden somewhere in the snow.

By the time Warren turned in toward the grove and the long driveway where they had parked so many nights and had made love, sometimes wild and passionately while at other times with great gentleness, both Jeanne and Warren were stiff and tense. Jeanne's eyes burned and her temples throbbed from the extreme concentration. She could imagine how exhausted Warren must be by now. In unspoken consent Warren passed their favorite parking spot in the grove, not even thinking as they passed that the entire driveway was filling with deep snow, and tonight it would have been impossible to pull the car to the side had they been of a mind to do so. Instead, he fought the car into the yard and parked along the hedge near the windmill.

Warren switched off the ignition and turned slightly, pulling Jeanne gently toward him. This was not to be a night for making love, but a night to feel safe in each other's arms, to share the comfort their love brought by just being together. "You'll have to come in, Warren. You know you're always welcome. It's too awful to even think of driving all the way to Montevideo."

For a moment, Warren's head lolled back against the seat. Even though the car was parked, his body seemed to float, still reacting to the vertigo caused by driving without being able to orient to familiar landmarks. "Yes, it really was foolish for us to go out tonight, wasn't it?" His head spun, and his stomach felt light. "It always seems like a good idea, when I think of the wonderful time we have together. A little thing like a blizzard could hardly keep us from being together, could it?" They clung gently to each other. Warren leaned forward, kissed her waiting lips as Jeanne snuggled close with her arms pressed around him. They were happy to be together and to be safe once more.

For a few moments they sat in the car thinking their private thoughts. Even here, in the protection of the grove, the frigid wind buffeted the car. Now they could hear the wind shrieking through the trees, and suddenly they both realized the magnitude, the frightening freezing power of the storm they had braved just to be together. As the car rapidly cooled the reality of the day-long blizzard came back to them.

Just barely visible through the storm was the light left as a dim beacon for Jeanne's return home. With their coats pulled tightly about them they slammed their doors and dashed for the porch. The heavy wet snow was above their knees, and twice Jeanne stumbled and fell, to have Warren grab her and propel her toward the house. Finally, they reached the safety of the house.

In the kitchen hall they shivered as they hung their coats by the door and put their wet shoes beneath the stove to dry by morning. After extinguishing the kitchen light they walked together to the living room, and settling onto the mohair couch, they clung together until they were sound asleep.

Jeanne woke the next morning to the smell of the fresh coffee and frying bacon on the kitchen stove. When her mother had risen and found the two still clinging together in their sleep she gave a silent prayer of thanks for their safety and spread a quilt over them.

Quietly now Jeanne slipped off the couch and while running fingers through her hair she joined her mother in the kitchen. Shortly after, Warren wakened, at the same time Jeanne's father and her brothers Henry and Peter returned from their morning chores, all three exclaiming loudly that the storm was still too fierce to be caught in. If not absolutely necessary, even the trip to the barn would have been happily postponed. Then, with much laughter and teasing of the still wrinkled young couple, they all enjoyed their hearty breakfast. As they sat over a last cup of coffee, discussing the storm still raging outside, Jeanne's nightmare began.

Even over the howling wind they all heard the large snowplow coming long before they saw it. The big International truck with the V-shaped plow ground slowly along the driveway. Occasionally, even in the bitter cold, sparks flew from beneath the huge blade as it scraped a cross the frozen rocky drive. The township maintained the roads throughout the area. It wasn't unusual for the snowplow to turn around in their yard before continuing its winter mission, but it never came through in the middle of a storm, and surely this storm was not over yet. Unanimously they stood and moved to the kitchen windows to look through the accumulated frost into the yard. Their surprise increased when what they saw was not the township plow. In the yard they saw the Chippewa County plow which must have come through the storm all the way from Montevideo. "What the heck?" Jeanne's pa exclaimed. The plow was turning from the yard and at the end of the plowed swath they saw the sheriff's blue Ford sedan. And stepping from the car were Sheriff Brown and two deputies.

The sheriff and one of the deputies moved to Warren's Dodge. The deputy opened the car's door, looked in for a moment while the sheriff skirted the car, looking at its tires, then made some comment to the sheriff which those in the house were unable to interpret. Closing the door to the storm the deputy joined his companions who were already wading through the blowing snow toward the house.

Before the sheriff and his men reached the house Jeanne's father strode to the kitchen door and swung it open. Grabbing the edge of the storm door to keep it from being caught by the wind, he leaned out into the chilly morning and yelled "Come in Sheriff, come in. It's too cold out there to stand on formality. Come in by the stove and get warmed up." He finished greeting the sheriff and his deputies, then stepped aside to allow them, stamping the snow from their feet, and loosening their coats about their shoulders, into the kitchen.

Jeanne knew if she lived to be a hundred she would never forget what took place in the next fifteen minutes. In a moment, the jovial mood which existed around the family table changed. There was tension in the air, for they all knew it must be serious business afoot to bring the sheriff and his deputies out on such a morning. "Sheriff, let me pour you come coffee," said Jeanne's mother. "It's a terrible morning to be out. You look like you've been out all night, and I'm not surprised, with a storm like this. What in the world brings you out to our farm this morning?"

"Thank you for the coffee, ma'am," responded Carl. "We're here on business, and I'm sure sorry to interrupt your Sunday breakfast. And we have been out all night. There was an accident on the county road west of Number Fifty-nine, on the road that goes down to Buster's and the big construction site where they're putting in the new dam." The cherubic smile he bent toward Mrs. Amundson was strained and his tired eyes flashed across the room.

"Oh, my," Jeanne's mother replied. "Don't tell me somebody went in the ditch during the night. How terrible that would be. It must have been twenty below during the night. How could anybody survive something like that?"

"Well, Missus, there was an accident over there, but it wasn't somebody drove into the ditch. As a matter of fact, if that had been it, my job would be easier now. You see, we had somebody hit by a car last night and left in a snowbank. We don't know yet if he was still alive when the car drove off and the poor fellow died from exposure, or if the car killed him outright. As it happened, I come up the hill right after the accident...if that's what it was. It looked to me that the man was killed outright, though." He turned slowly as he continued. "And I'm sure sorry I have to insult your hospitality folks, but the car that hit the man is the one Warren was driving."

"Oh, that's not possible, Sheriff," said Jeanne. "It couldn't be."

"That can't be, Sheriff! Surely Jeanne and I would have known if we'd hit someone," Warren spoke as he stood from the table.

"Just take it easy young man; sit back down," replied the sheriff. "I was just inside Buster's when you and Jeanne left a little after eleven last night. As a matter of fact I was just inside the door talking to another couple when I saw you drive out. I saw you as you hit that patch of ice and go fishtailing when you reached the road. I was a little concerned, "because I'd seen you had been drinking a lot in the evening. You might remember I commented you should watch it on a night like last night, and that it wouldn't do to be out in this cold with a belly full of liquor."

"Being concerned about your well-being as I was, I decided maybe I ought to head out in case something happened to you. I figured once you got past highway fifty-nine you were going to be okay. Well, I didn't see any other cars come up that hill after you left, and I didn't see any other cars come down the hill either. There wasn't a sign of a car but yours. I remember thinking as I left Buster's that it'd take a mighty damn fool to go out on a night like last night if they didn't have to. I don't know for the life of me what all the folks were doing at Buster's. I guess we should feel lucky that transient is the only one dead from a storm like this."

"When all is said, I got into my car and headed up the hill. I'd decided if you made it as far as highway fifty-nine I was going to head into Montevideo and call it a night. The way the storm was going, the odds were pretty good I was going to be called out before the night was over. As I came up the hill, busting through the snow banks the only tracks ahead of me was the ones you made, sometimes on the right side and sometimes on the left; I don't know if it was because of your drinking, Warren, or if you were just trying to get through the drifts. Then, just out by the Carlson's grove I saw this black object sticking out of the snow. When I jumped out to see what it was, I gave it a pull. I thought it might have been a scarf or a mitten one of you fool kids somehow dropped out of the car, but I came up with the hand of this dead transient inside his black mackinaw."

"Well, a person doesn't have to go far from there to figure what happened. I woke the Carlson's after I put out some flares to be sure nobody coming up the hill ran into the back of my Ford. Then I called my deputy in Montevideo and before he could get out there he had to get the county plow, since the road all the way to

Montevideo was already drifted shut. I'm not sure how you got to this farm young man, 'cause there sure is snow stacked up everyplace across the county right now."

"Well, during the course of the night we got that fellow unburied, brought him into the Carlson's porch, and laid him out to see who he was, to find out what identification he had on him, and just see what we could see."

"I had a good look at the tracks in the snow, the tracks that went across his body. They're the same tracks as on your tires, Warren. So I'm going to have to take you in. Maybe when we sit down and analyze this we'll find there was nothing you could do to keep from hitting that man, but in the meantime it's still hit and run and it looks like, from all the evidence I see, that you're going to end up being charged with manslaughter."

"But...but..." sputtered Jeanne, "I was with Warren. I know he didn't hit anybody. If you're taking him in take me too. I know we didn't hit anybody."

"Jeanne, I know how fond you are of Warren, and I know you were with him last night, but there's no reason for you to leave your warm home on a day like today. You weren't driving the car, so in the worst case you aren't going to be under arrest. You certainly couldn't be blamed for Warren's hitting that man. But Warren's going to have to come in. We can leave his car here or have one of my deputies drive it in if it'll start."

Jeanne's dad stepped forward. "Sheriff, isn't there anything we can do? You and I both know Warren's a good man. I've known his family all his life. And I know you've seen Warren from time to time working around the county. You know he's reliable. I just find this hard to believe, Sheriff."

"So do I," responded Carl. There was no smile now, his hard brown eyes focused on Warren. "But the fact is, my hands are tied. It was Warren's car that ran over that man and I have to take Warren in."

"Well, Sheriff, if you leave Warren's car here we'll see it's driven in. There's no need to put more cars on the road in this weather than necessary. Warren, don't you worry. I'll get hold of your folks, and we'll see this gets cleared up and taken care of immediately."

All this time Warren had remained speechless. Oh, sure, he knew Sheriff Brown didn't like him, but he couldn't believe the sheriff would try to blame something like this on him. There must be some mistake. So, quietly Warren went along. "Don't worry, Jeanne. This will be over in no time," he said now. "There's no way I can be found guilty of whatever it is the sheriff is trying to say." Gathering his coat about him and taking his gloves from the top of the kitchen stove Warren hugged Jeanne close. With tears in her eyes Jeanne watched from the kitchen window as the sheriff's car took Warren away.

CHAPTER

SEVENTEEN
March 7, 1938

They stood silently by the grave as the minister read the last rites for Timmy. Tom Hall, who had come only to claim his brother's body, and Jeanne, who now leaned on him for support, stood apart from the others, and they were shedding no tears. To Jeanne the gathering seemed surreal, and to Tom, a stranger to all those present, it was just another sad moment in his odyssey to bring Ernie home. The dark sky was threatening another thunderstorm and the cold wind whipped around Jeanne's legs and across her back. Even with her long wool coat pulled tight around her Jeanne couldn't stop a chill from shivering through her body.

"Ashes to ashes," intoned the minister. He looked briefly at the two of them standing motionless. "Dust to dust…"

"What an awful way to die," Jeanne thought. "I'm not sure, even with all the pain and violence Timmy had caused, that he deserved to die like that." Then, as they walked from the gravesite across the muddy ground, Tom took her by the elbow, steadying her as they turned their backs to the somber crowd.

"How pale she is," Tom thought to himself as they moved toward the car. "What an ordeal she's been through." And as an afterthought "How sad that my brother died for so little a cause."

Now that it was ended ,Tom knew he could board the train and go back home to Ohio, leaving this little town forever. Jeanne, however, must pick up the pieces of her life and put hate and the death and violence behind her.

As they passed through the stone gates of Memorial Cemetery the cold rain started once again. Tom switched on the windshield wipers and they drove slowly back into town. He was driving Warren's Dodge; the family insisted. Occasionally he looked over at Jeanne, who seemed to be in a trance. Her eyes were glassy and her skin was pale and waxy. Sitting motionless beside Tom, she looked very tiny and frail, and he wondered that she stood up to the ordeal so well.

As the wipers continued their steady click...click...click, in harmony with the small electric motor overhead which drove the wiper blades against the rain a shiver went up Tom's spine as he realized this was the car which had probably caused his brother's death. Sitting as if hypnotized, Jeanne's mind was wandering back to the beginning of the nightmare, which seemed to have no end.

"How wonderfully that night had begun," she recalled. After a mostly pleasant time she and Warren had left Buster's, both finally ready to leave their friends behind for another night.

As they left the roadhouse Warren had his arm wrapped across the shoulders of her heavy wool coat and hugged her close in a boozy lust. Although Jeanne too, felt amorous, she was still upset over the near fight from which Warren had just been pulled. Sometimes she couldn't understand why men were such jerks, willing to spoil everything by fighting. Thank heaven enough of their friends stepped in before Warren and Timmy really had time to get into it.

Cuddling close in the dark, they hugged and kissed while Warren's car warmed enough to start defrosting the windshield. Jeanne let his hand wander inside the heavy coat, squeezing and caressing her breasts. It wasn't the first time; she enjoyed the caressing as much as he. Inside her, it felt like a feather that was being lightly brushed the length of her body, tingling, and quivering its way across her stomach and into her panties, sending little spasms, which Warren could never experience, through her entire being.

When Warren buried his face inside the neck of her dress Jeanne wanted to throw caution to the wind and love him right there in the parking lot beside Buster's. But she knew better; now it would be only good for him; wham, bam, thank you Jeanne. Later, parked in the grove along the driveway to her parents' farm she would slow him down so they'd both enjoy the sex together—booze or not.

"Honey let's head for the farm," she whispered, reluctantly pulling herself away and pushing his hands from beneath her coat. "I don't want anyone to catch us, and it'll be better in the grove when your car's warmed up."

As they drove out of the lot at Buster's the wind whipped the snow viciously, sometimes totally blocking their vision. For a while Jeanne had forgotten about the raging storm. Now she didn't like the looks of it, but Warren just laughed as the wheels of his Dodge spun and the little car's rear end fishtailed as the tires dug through the snow cover and hit an icy spot on the road. Jeanne knew Warren was thinking more about being parked in the grove with her dress opened from top to bottom and her legs wrapped tightly around his hard hips, than he was about how dangerous the drive to the farm was going to be.

In second gear Warren revved the car up the hill, much too fast already for Jeanne, who was just a little more sober than Warren. As they bumped and thumped their way through the drifts up the long hill leading home Jeanne, friendly but persistently, pushed Warren's attention away from her breasts and back to driving. On previous nights she had enjoyed and even joined Warren in such mobile foreplay as they crossed toward her home, but tonight's weather had her worried and she wanted Warren to concentrate on driving.

Hot air channeling upward from the defroster scribed soft patterns across the windshield and the humming of the engine lulled the couple; even the whooshing of tires plowing through the wide deep snow drifts seemed to almost tranquilize them as they drove. Even though the snow and wind buffeted the little coupe, it was difficult to concentrate, to acknowledge the existence of the storm.

In the middle of a mutual love peck neither of them noticed that one of drifts they hit sounded quite different than those before and after it. Neither heard the crunch of bones being broken by the two cold hard sixteen inch tires. Neither of them had even an inclination to look back, so Warren and Jeanne didn't see the man lying in their tire track, already partly covered with blowing snow, his ragged coat whipping stiffly in the wintry night wind. They were busy, in love and lusting, impatiently making the long trip to the grove.

"Oh, yes," Jeanne smiled at the thought. "...the grove." The grove was satisfactory anytime, but in the summer, and throughout the year when it was warm and dry, Warren and Jeanne had other special places as well. The hillside overlooking the lake, when there was a breeze so the mosquitoes didn't leave giant welts on them both from one end to the other, which they had learned the hard way, was such a place, and on sweltering summer evenings when Ma and Pa thought they were walking down by the lake, they liked to sneak into the hayloft. There was something especially erotic, she thought, about being naked with Warren in the hayloft. The heavy musty smell of the livestock below, combined with the smell of the freshly gathered hay covering their bodies, increased her lust for him. Covered with sweat, they both became like the other barn animals, and rutted for the sheer pleasure of their violent climaxes, moaning with ecstasy in the privacy of the great hayloft. Then later they giggled like kids as they picked off the hay that stuck to their bodies everywhere. Sometimes touching each other while they picked off the hay made them both too excited and they'd fall into another deep spasm of lovemaking.

But right now it was different; it was January, 1938, and it was twelve degrees below zero. It was eight miles to her parents' farm from Buster's, and with all the snow which had been falling since mid-morning, Jeanne was afraid they might have a very long trip to the farm. In every protected area and alongside each farm grove there were deep drifts of snow, many covering the entire road, causing Warren's Dodge to shudder, and to lurch, as if some great white hand were trying to pull them to a stop in the frigid white night.

When the snow had started earlier in the day it had been twenty degrees above zero and the first flakes had been heavy and wet, sticking where they fell. It has been the kind of snow Jeanne had always dreamed of for Christmas. The big evergreens along the driveway at home were sagging under the new weight of heavy snow, and already covered by several snowfalls this winter, the farm's outbuildings had drifts nearly to the roofs.

As the day progressed the temperatures began to drop, and with the dropping temperature the snowflakes became smaller and harder. On occasion, while walking to the barn, Jeanne was hit by a sudden gust of icy wind which slammed the hard snow against her face. But even the continuing snow and the deteriorating weather couldn't chill Jeanne's excitement. This was Saturday, the night she and Warren spent together. After her chores, snow or no snow, Warren would be guiding his old Dodge coupe through the grove and they would soon be on their way to town.

CHAPTER
EIGHTEEN
March 9, 1938

Tom and Jeanne were deep in their private thoughts as Tom drove along Main Street. Tom, now that this strange adventure was coming to its climax, was thinking of his return to Ohio, while Jeanne could think of nothing but the relief of having Warren free from jail, of having her life back. She now was able to find comfort in remembering how she and Warren had come to be together and so much in love. The simple routine of farm life had changed for her since Warren had entered her life.

It was still Jeanne's job to feed the chickens and gather their eggs before supper each day. In the summer she also did this in the morning. Her brothers also had their chores. Feeding the hogs and throwing hay down for the horses at one end of the barn, then putting feed into their feed boxes, which was usually Henry's job.

Henry liked this time of day, when he could talk to all the horses, calling them by name as he dumped grain from the bucket into their feed boxes. Then, if he hadn't dawdled too long already, he liked to sit on the back of Dan, the big bay Belgian, for a while before his chores called him back.

The sounds of the eight large draft horses chewing, rubbing against their stalls, sighing, and shaking their halters as they fed was Henry's most cherished reward for a hard day's work.

Jeanne liked to join Henry at this peaceful time of day, lying on the broad back of her favorite mare, Daisy, who she had raised from a foal. Henry didn't know, however, that recently while Jeanne was lying there on her stomach, legs stretched across the mare's back and rocking back and forth, that she was thinking mostly of Warren and that lying here like this felt almost as good as having him between her legs.

While Henry took care of the horses Jeanne's other brothers, Peter, and Eddie, fed hay to the cows through a chute in the other end of the barn, forking great piles of hay to the floor, then placing a huge forkful or two in front of each cow standing chained in her stanchion. They also gave the cows a large scoop of grain and fed them this way twice a day, every day of the year.

When there was a new calf, it suckled for a week or so to get the first lactose-rich mild from its mother. Then, the calf was put with the others in a large pen, one of several at the end of the barn, where it learned to drink from a bucket, then later to eat hay and grain.

Sometimes Jeanne helped feed the calves. She liked those times, especially with the new calves, for the new calves had to learn to drink from the bucket. Jeanne allowed the hungry calf to suck on her fingers, its tongue rasping like coarse sandpaper as she slowly lowered her hand into the warm fresh milk. Then as the calf began to draw milk from the bucket she slowly withdrew her hand.

When the men were busy with field work Jeanne did some of the milking. But, in the winter they didn't milk as many cows of course, and she got by with taking care of the chickens and helping her ma in the house. On Saturdays everyone seemed to work a little faster. This was the night they'd all go to town.

From the time she and her brothers were little they'd all gone into Watson together on Saturday nights. It was the night for shopping and seeing all the friends who had also been busy during the week. The few stores, the locker plant, and the café which usually closed at six o'clock the rest of the week stayed open on Saturday night for their farm trade.

Pa would drive the Model A Ford, which he'd bought second-hand a couple of years ago, but she remembered going the four miles in their wagon all the while she was growing up. She didn't recall they'd ever had a buggy since they weren't too well off, but her grandparents had always had a beautiful buggy with big shiny wheels and a black top. It even had side curtains, and sometimes after he'd had a few drinks Pa would start to talk about pulling those curtains closed when he was courting Ma and they parked in the grove. Ma always scolded him, with a gleam in her eye Jeanne thought, and Pa never finished telling the story. Jeanne wondered that her folks might ever have felt the way she and Warren did about each other.

Jeanne no longer rode to town with her parents. Last summer she had met Warren and soon he had started coming by for her on Saturday nights. They didn't actually meet for the first time just last summer; they grew up right there within a few miles of each other. But Warren had been gone off and on for several years. Then, suddenly there he was, playing horseshoes in the lot next to the fire hall one Saturday when she and her folks drove by. In the span of one evening her life changed.

The last time she'd seen Warren he had been fifteen. He'd just finished the ninth grade then and they were worlds apart. Ninth graders were the oldest kids in school. After graduating from country school some went to high school in Milan, or maybe even in Montevideo {Monte to most people}, but most of the boys left school after the sixth grade since lots of folks still thought more schooling was a waste when the young people were needed for farm work.

When Warren finished ninth grade he went to work for his grandfather, who had a big farm north of Watson. Even though there was always work to be done these were trying times and putting Warren to work was part need and part family duty. Warren, and later his sister Abbe, worked and lived with their grandparents. It eased the hard times for Warren's and Abbe's folks and gave the children some chance to earn a living until times got better. Like most farm families, they were still trying to recover from the drought years and the depression following the big stock market crash in 1929.

After working for his grandfather for a couple of years Warren left the farm, and eventually took a job driving truck in Montevideo. Although he still came home to his parents for Sunday dinner most weeks, Jeanne hadn't seen him since he graduated from ninth grade. It seemed like forever. It seemed like yesterday. Now here he was, a tall curly haired hunk of good looking guy. If it were possible, he was even better looking than before, when she had such a horrible crush on him. Now she knew immediately that this was the boy for her. Her very first; her last too, she was sure.

So, on Saturday she left her parents at the grain elevator where they parked the car, Ma to get groceries and Pa stopping by the blacksmith before heading for Arnie's Pool Hall, where he would spend the evening drinking beer with his friends while they shot pool and talked about the problems of farm life.

Jeanne headed directly for the horseshoe yard. Although she usually spent Saturday nights walking around Watson with her friend Dolly, tonight she wanted to be alone, and was almost angry when Dolly spotted her. Talking a mile a minute about all the most recent gossip Dolly just couldn't be given the slip.

It didn't take Jeanne long to know Warren had spotted her as she and Dolly stood watching the horseshoe game. Warren's near-perfect horseshoe game turned into a rout as time and again he widely missed his toss. Finally Warren threw his hands in the air and left in disgust, leaving his opponents cheering while his partner was left, trying to figure out what was happening.

During the next few weeks Warren and Jeanne saw each other on Saturdays in Watson. Dolly, at first slow to take the hint, soon realized she had become a third foot when, talking as usual while the three walked toward the softball field, she turned toward Jeanne only to find herself alone with her bag of popcorn.

Before long, Warren was coming by the farm on Sunday afternoons. At first, Warren was welcomed by Mrs. Amundson with a degree of hesitancy. Warren's move to Montevideo, and his reputation as a regular at Buster's Roadhouse made the Amundsons a little nervous, but his presence was accepted before summer was over. Jeanne and Warren had become an item, spending every available hour together.

Suddenly, Jeanne's reverie was interrupted and she was yanked back to the present by the deep baritone of Tom's voice beside her. "My train leaves in just a couple of hours. If it's all right with you I'll drop you off and take the car to the depot." Since their second meeting Tom had been driving Warren's coupe. At first he had been uncomfortable behind the wheel of the auto which had run over Ernie, but Jeanne had insisted, and it had solved transportation problems for him. The fact was, within only a few days Tom hardly thought of the coupe and Ernie as being connected. "I'll leave the keys in the car at the depot; I'm sure no one will bother the car."

"I'm sure that will be fine, Tom. I wish there were more I could say or do. We'll arrange to get the car later."

"I hope things will go well for you now that this is cleared up, Jeanne, and although my brother is dead I'm glad I was able to help you."

Moments later Tom stopped in front of a large brick building and waited as Jeanne slammed the door and ran through the rain. For a few moments he sat and watched absently as she disappeared into the cavernous Montgomery Ward department store. Then, dropping the shift lever in to first gear he crept once again along the street.

"Man, oh man, how different this all might have been if I hadn't shown up," he thought. "Isn't it strange how chanced will sometimes intervene with fate."

CHAPTER
NINETEEN

Three men sat quietly in the corner of the bar. It was just another night, like any other winter evening where men gathered. While others around them seemed in a festive mood, possibly left over from the recent holiday season, those three men were quietly engaged in serious conversation.

The bar's other occupants seldom paid any attention to the three swarthy complexioned men. Although they were not strangers here, their presence was merely tolerated, rather than accepted. The eldest man at the table was known as John Walking Bear, most often called Uncle by the two young men with him. It was John Walking Bear who was now speaking.

"You must not let your anger control your thoughts, my sons." Although they were not really his sons, he thought of them as such since both of them had been raised like sons, since their infancy, by John Walking Bear and his wife while she still lived. They had been part of John Walking Bear's daily life since they were infants.

"It is the way of the white man. You would think after all of these years he would learn to treat us well, wouldn't you? But it seems it is only our women they lust after. They don't see the women as we see them of course, but only as animals; to be used, then discarded. But control your anger, and the time will come when we see justice served."

"I would kill him," hissed one of the younger men. John Walking Bear knew he would have to keep an eye on this one, whose anger was too near the surface; his memories were fanned like hot coals, by the actions at the bar. "I would like to gut him like a deer and leave him in the alley like the vermin he is. See how he looks at her Uncle; how he runs his filthy hands across her legs."

"No, William," responded John Walking Bear. "You must remember that she sits there of her own free will. And if you should fight him, if you should kill him where would your victory be? You know that man is the sheriff in Chippewa County now. No matter what a bad man we know him to be, if harm should come to him the law will punish us. Where would the victory be then?"

"But look at him, Uncle," William grumbled again. "I cannot bear to look. Uh. How can she stand to let him insult her so?"

In many taverns and social gathering places across the valley, young and old men alike watched while white men pursued the Indian women, saw the treatment of their women by the whites as degrading, a continuation of the inequity that had plagued them for a century. Sometimes cooler heads such as John Walking Bear's prevailed; other times they did not.

"Perhaps it is the liquor that speaks in you. But keep a clear head." Through the afternoon the three men had sat in the tavern. Like many others they drank Coca Cola laced with moonshine from the bottle in the plain brown wrapper. But John Walking Bear, unlike his two young companions, had drank hardly at all; mostly Coca Cola, for he knew the danger of drinking too much liquor and was there as much to keep the two youths out of trouble as he was for the entertainment.

It was a sad thing which had happened over the years to his people, to become dependent on the white man's liquor and to see the families slide deeper and deeper into poverty, to see their health deteriorate. His own wife had been a victim of tuberculosis, which had been unknown to them before the white man came into their valley. Now he lived with these two men he thought of his as sons in a small cabin alongside the Minnesota River.

On winter days such as today they would drive to Montevideo, or as they had done today, drive to Boyd, where they would sit in the spacious tavern talking as men will always talk. Talking of the good old days, fishing in the river, and catching sauger and catfish and sturgeon, of the men they had known and the adventures they had shared, they would pleasantly pass the winter day.

But on some days, like this one, their pleasure was dampened when such men as Carl Brown came to fondle and caress one of their women, to take them off to the bush or the back seat of their car as these men so often did.

As he watched Carl Brown pawing and groping, putting moves on the young woman at the bar he was angry just as William was. But John Walking Bear knew that a patient man would eventually have his revenge. After all, didn't the Indian know that in the end justice would always be done. John Walking Bear had learned to be patient.

While John Walking Bear carefully watched the man at the bar, he regaled his two young companions again with tales of the hunt, stories that told of his youth, when buffalo could still found on Minnesota's prairies and when deer were plentiful along the river. He told them—for perhaps the hundredth time—of trapping the muskrat and the mink and the weasel along the banks of the river.

He told again of the blizzards that came through the river valley leaving snow as high as a man was tall. He told again the legends which had passed from father to son for generations by the Sioux. And he retold stories from a time when they were a free and proud people, not living in squalid cabins on the agency where they were considered second or even third class citizens by the farmers and townsmen who settled along the Minnesota River. In his soft voice, John Walking Bear tried to soothe his young charges with peaceful stories, to keep their passions from taking command of their minds, but he knew that he himself had not always been so peaceful. There was at time long past when like William, he would have sought the immediate justice of his knife.

John Walking Bear knew the young woman at the bar would eventually go off into the night with Carl Brown, plied with liquor and fancy words, hoping to be loved and cared for, hoping this man would see her for the proud beautiful woman she was. She would go with him, to be defiled and left behind as Carl Brown had left others over the years. Some of those women had been badly beaten and all had been ridiculed and rejected by him in the end.

As he watched, John Walking Bear thought again of the proper punishment for a man who defiled the woman of his family, who stripped them of their honor and self-respect. As he looked sadly into the empty glass twirling between his gnarly fingers he reverted to his native Dakotah as he told his young companions how their people had dealt with such men as the one they now so painfully watched.

CHAPTER

TWENTY

February 20, 1938

On this night John Walking Bear sat alone, quietly nursing a cup of coffee, his mind filled with the memories of his life. As he sat, he watched across the room, where Carl Brown pressed himself against the young Indian girl at his side.

Sitting in a booth in the back of the tavern, Carl Brown was gloriously drunk. As he roared and raved like a madman he seemed to John Walking Bear like a mad dog. One moment he was viciously kissing the young woman pressed into the corner beside him, the next swinging his glass high and shouting vulgarities to those sitting at the bar. Carl Brown epitomized all that John Walking Bear despised in a man whether he be red or white.

John Walking Bear had lived here in the valley of the Minnesota River all of his life—nearly seventy years. The changes which had taken place along the river in his lifetime could not be counted. Not all of the changes were good, he knew.

As a boy he had roamed through the woods and had ridden his pony through the rocky valleys which fed tiny streams into the Minnesota River. He recalled that once he had scared a family of white settlers who came through the valley when, on a dare by the other boys, he had ridden his pony at a full gallop right toward their covered wagon screaming as loud as he could. They all went scurrying for safety, fearing an attack until he veered away at the last minute and they saw their attacker was only a ten year old boy.

That night as he related his victory tale his father smiled sadly before scolding John Walking Bear. "The white families who come do not find humor when you count coup on them in this manner. To many of them we are savage animals; they have not forgotten how fiercely he fought here for our land not many years ago.

Yes, John Walking Bear recalled that it was not so very many years ago death and fear had filled the valleys of the Minnesota River. His own father had been sixteen years old when the great uprising had taken place in the new state of Minnesota and had himself fought against the white settlers.

For a long while before the uprising the white man's government had abused the Dakotah who had made these valleys their home. Making everyone live on the agency land was an insult in itself, since the proud Dakotah had always chosen where they would live. But restricting them to the agency lands had almost brought an end to these proud people.

The cold winters had taken their toll on many families, since they were no longer allowed to follow the buffalo, to kill enough buffalo and deer to provide winter food. And now, finally, the buffalo were gone. The food promised by the Agency manager did not arrive and many starved. In the spring many young men wanted to strike back, but the elders had prevailed for a while.

Then in the summer of 1862, four Wahpeton braves had killed two families of settlers in Acton Township. This action by Killing Ghost and his friends had ignited the warriors' fires and for many days the angry Dakota and the white settlers had killed each other. Near Redwood Falls the Dakotah braves had ambushed and killed nearly a whole platoon of soldiers before being driven off, while at Monson Lake, near New London, thirteen members of a single family were slain. Many settlements, such as New Ulm, Wood Lake, and others across Minnesota, were saved from destruction only by the modern weapons the governor sent with General Sibley and his soldiers from Fort Snelling.

All across the new state of Minnesota fires burned in the night, where the brave warriors wrought vengeance until the last great battle was fought at Birch Coulee, and the fighting was brought to a bloody end. The fierceness and effectiveness of the Dakotah was brought to light for settlers living around the upper agency when in a great ceremony the Dakotah released two hundred sixty-nine prisoners, women, children, and people of mixed blood, near Montevideo.

But in the end, the white man had prevailed, and the Indians were once more returned to a life of privation and disdain by those he had fought bravely against. Over three hundred braves were to be hanged, to set an example for those who remained, but the great President Lincoln had spoken for the Indians and finally on December 26, 1862, the day after Christmas, only thirty-nine died on the white man's gallows. Although John Walking Bear's father was not one of those, there were many from his family whose cold corpses had swayed stiffly in the wind.

Unlike many of the white men living in the valley today John Walking Bear did not hold a grudge for that which was so long past. He knew there had been good things to come with the white settlers as well as the bad.

He had seen the coming of the railroad and he had been present when the first steam driven automobile had hissed and puffed its way through the valley. The valley had no paved road in those days, and the automobiles had to follow the same primitive roadways used for horse drawn wagons. At first people had been frightened, and the horses, startled by the fearsome noise, were uncontrollable. As the driver fought his ridiculous machine through potholes and over rocks, John Walking Bear and others had begun to laugh at the foolish sight. While others, driving teams of horses, enjoyed the pleasant spring day in their shirtsleeves, this strange traveler was bundled in a great coat, which covered him to his knees, with a scarf about his neck and goggled cap to protect his eyes. When he had passed, the onlookers had formed a line, squatting as if about to dump their toilet, and waddled about making vulgar noises, "sh't, sh't, th'rt, th'rt!" like pissing and farting on dry basswood leaves.

Before the new century arrived, John Walking Bear had taken a wife, the daughter of his father's cousin who lived further down the valley near Morton. They had two children who had not survived their tenth birthdays, dying of smallpox when an epidemic had swept through the valley leaving many empty beds and empty hearts behind. In 1931 his lovely wife died at the age of fifty-six, leaving John Walking Bear's life empty except for William, his brother's only son and Jonathon Crow, who was a great grandson of the brave warrior Little Crow.

John Walking Bear and his wife had considered these two almost as children of their own, nurturing and teaching them as many of the traditional ways as they could. The young men's respect showed in their always deferential treatment and in the respected title of Uncle, which both young men used when addressing him.

Although many Dakota men and women had lost much of their self-respect, John Walking Bear had brought the two young men to adulthood with a sense of self-worth and pride in their heritage. They watched as some around them wallowed in self-pity and anger toward the whites they blamed for all their problems. While both of the young men sometimes drank too much moonshine, they usually responded to John Walking Bear's admonitions and refrained from drunkenness.

John Walking Bear felt a sense of relief that his two nephews were not with him tonight. Recently they had been hard pressed to restrain their anger when they saw how some of the whites treated the Indian women, and he did not blame either of them for their show of anger. They wanted only equal treatment, and justice, as men all over have always wanted.

He knew, however, that it was hard for any man to show respect toward another who regularly submitted to drunkenness, as did the young woman seated in the corner with Carl Brown. But even she should receive common respect given to a woman. To Carl Brown however, respect was not a word even related to any Indian.

John Walking Bear knew that Carl Brown seldom paid any attention to him whenever they might meet, but especially on a night like this, when the Chippewa County sheriff was drunk, and thinking only of the throbbing member in his pants. He knew that hour after hour the sheriff would press himself on the young girl, and when her defenses were weakest, his lust at its peak, this man would take the girl to his car. He would promise her a ride home. Somehow the young women from the

Sioux Agency could not resist the lure of this man. But on the way home he would detour into the deep woods beside the river.

It would not matter if she objected, for Carl Brown would beat her into submission if need be, then have his way with her. If she angered him enough he would throw her out of the car and throw her clothes in the bushes, leaving her crying, to find her way home in the night.

Although John Walking Bear sat alone, others from the agency were also in the tavern and at a nearby table sat two young men known to John Walking Bear. In the space of a moment, the two Indian boys jumped angrily to their feet. They had been drinking for some time John Walking Bear knew, and as they watched Carl's distasteful antics their bile had continued to rise. Now, unable to contain themselves any longer they struck out at the man who, in their eyes, was forcing his attention on the young woman.

They pushed threateningly against the booth as Carl released his hold on the girl. There was contempt in Carl's eyes. "Alright Boys, alright; I thought she wanted my attention." There was a sinister gleam in his eye as he continued, "After all she was welcome to leave anytime she wanted, wasn't she?"

"There's no need to start any trouble," Carl said as he slid away from the girl. At the edge of the booth he twisted his body as he started to rise.

"There's no need to make a scene," he repeated apologetically. "I'll just slide out of here and you young fellows can sit down and find out whether she really wanted my attention or not."

With their guards relaxed now by his repentant voice, the young men didn't see Carl's hand lash out. His hands had remained protected from their sight by the breadth of his body and they didn't see him grab the coke bottle in front of him. With lightning fast movements Carl swung the bottle, catching the nearest man on the side of the jaw. Then he lunged before either man could react. With his massive weight behind him he threw his shoulder into the chest of the second man who went sprawling across the adjoining table.

While the first man was still trying to recover from the vicious blow from the bottle Carl gave him a vicious kick to the ribs and he fell screaming to the floor. Then, standing flat footed, with his arms akimbo, his hate filled eyes bore into the two young men.

"If you two sons of bitches think you're going to intimidate me you've got another think coming. You lazy bastards think you can come in here and scare me…well, forget it. This bitch has been after me for a long time. Don't you think I know that? Now, drag your red tails back to the reservation and don't bother me again."

In the first moment of the brawl John Walking bear had half raised from the chair. Then he settled back for it was over as fast as it had begun. The two men had been unprepared for Carl's vicious attack. John Walking Bear knew that to enter into the argument at this point would only be disastrous. His hands pressed tightly around his cup as he watched Carl grab the young woman by the arm.

"Let's get the hell out of here," Carl growled contemptuously as he pushed the young woman out the door into the night.

The two defeated men gathered themselves when Carl was gone. As they helped one another to the door they glared at John Walking Bear and swore at his cowardice for not assisting them. They blamed their defeat not on their own foolishness, but on John Walking Bear's failure to assist them. He, saddened by their anger, averted his eyes as they passed.

As he sat alone with his coffee, John Walking Bear knew that soon his time for patience would expire and that the time for the serving of justice would rule instead.

CHAPTER

TWENTY-ONE
February 24, 1938

As he sat alone in his quiet office Carl smiled as he thought about his progress; it seemed to Carl that his case against Warren was coming together nicely. Yes, there were still some ragged spots to cover, like finding conclusive proof connecting Warren to Timmy's death, but to Carl that seemed a minor and very solvable problem. *It's lucky,* he thought, *how I came along right after that son of a bitch got ran over. Hell, in a little, while he'd have been covered with so much snow that no one would have found him until the snowplow came by. No telling how I could ever solve his death.* Carl knew that if the body hadn't been discovered until after the storm—if he hadn't been right behind Warren—that the transient's death would just have been written off. No one was going to miss a damn transient. *Let him rot there for all I care.*

It gave Carl a pleasant glow however as he recalled how easily he had been able to solve the transient's death and that of Timmy Coyle. It was about like the movie he had seen at the Hollywood Theatre, Night Club Scandal, only instead of John Barrymore, it was Carl who was the hero. It was Carl ferreting out clues, risking his life while following faint trails that led to the killer. As he smiled at his own image reflected from a framed picture over his desk, Carl's thoughts drifted back to January 29th, and the events which all began at Buster's.

Carl left the boisterous roadhouse only a few minutes after Jeanne and Warren had driven into the stormy night. Unlike the others who left Buster's on such a frosty night, Carl didn't climb into a cold car. His car was left idling, so it was warm and toasty whenever he decided to leave. No matter where he was or how long he stayed, Carl felt he deserved a warm car. *The taxpayers can afford it,* was Carl's attitude. If he had to workday and night all over the damn county he at least deserved a warm car to climb into. And one that was dependable, too.

The sheriff's car was 1938 Ford. New, and it was what he knew he deserved. He'd talked the county board into this sweet little machine last fall. That flock of old fools wanted him on the job so bad they'd probably kiss his ass if that's what it took to keep him here. The image that conjured up brought a smile to Carl's face.

The little Ford was slick and fast with its eighty-five horsepower V-8 motor. The mohair seats were just about as comfortable as being at home on his couch. If he couldn't be home nice and warm, he believed his car should keep him as comfortable as possible as the bastion of law and order he deserved the best. Besides, being forced to drive his old Studebaker was bad for his image as sheriff, undermined his authority. Now, when Carl approached in his Ford everyone knew right away somebody important was coming.

Even though Carl left the heater and defroster on, he had to brush nearly a foot of snow off the Ford's hood and kick snow away from the door before he could get behind the wheel. Finally settled, he reached under the seat for the bottle he kept there "for medicinal purposes," took a hot slug then capped and returned the bottle to its safe refuge. He eased the Ford into second gear and slowly let out the clutch as he revved the engine, creeping ahead into the deep snow. Any fool knew better than try pulling out in the snow and ice in first gear. In this snow you'd have no control and you'd just spin your wheels looking like a fool. Carl was no fool.

Turning left onto the roadway Carl saw ahead of him the faint tracks of Warren's Dodge, already drifting shut as the howling wind stirred the falling snow. "What a bitch of a night. I imagine we'll have these damn farmers in every ditch from Milan to Wegdahl, probably find some of them froze to death, too fucking stupid to stay home on a night like this."

As he crept up the long hill Carl thought about the altercation which took place earlier between Timmy Coyle and Warren. "Asshole. I almost got him, too. If I'd gotten Warren to the car he'd have a busted skull to go with his smart mouth."

By the time Carl had entered the roadhouse earlier in the evening it was already buzzing with several dozen people, mostly locals who felt they were close enough to home that the storm was little threat. Mixed among the crowd were a few men from the transient camp across the road, but they kept to themselves, not feeling a real part of the community. There were also several faces he recognized from Montevideo, and from Dawson. "These damn fools must be crazy to come this far in this kind of weather," Carl thought as he worked his way through the crowd.

Warren and Jeanne, like most of the young couples, were dancing. Around them the air was thick with the smells of smoke, sweaty bodies, and stale booze.

Over the booths cigarette smoke hung like a heavy blue cloud. The air was hot and close, nearly a hundred degrees hotter than the frigid temperature just outside the door.

In one corner of the roadhouse the band was re-tuning between numbers. Three or four local farmers usually came on Saturday nights, playing old-time music the locals enjoyed, and they were here tonight in spite of the raging storm. Mazurkas, schottisches, and waltzes were mixed with a healthy number of polkas. Personally, Carl couldn't stand listening to very much of their music and thought most of it sounded like shit, he often said to his deputies. The longer they played the drunker the band got and by the end of the night he just couldn't stand it. Tonight Eddie and Palmer Roison, father, and son, who farmed together up by Big Bend, were sawing away at their fiddles. *Squalling like cats,* Carl thought, as he watched them stomping their feet to keep time. They were hunched over and looked to Carl like two drunken apes taking a crap, flailing their arms to show everybody where the piles were. Sig Engebretson stood in back torturing the hell out of his accordion.

All night Sig chewed on a big White Owl cigar, and between songs nipped at a bottle of liquor he kept by his feet. Carl couldn't figure out how Sig managed, but at closing time he was always still standing there, cigar in his mouth and his wild red hair springing out in every direction.

By eleven o'clock the noise level was enough to burst your eardrums, Carl remembered. He became continuously more irritated as he watched Warren dancing and smooching with Jeanne. Between dances now they just clung together, Warren's hands occasionally slipping to caress Jeanne's round bottom, both oblivious of everything and everyone else in the place. It was easy for Carl to see who expected to get laid tonight. "Son of a bitch," Carl mused to himself.

Then, just as Carl was thinking of leaving, it looked like things were going to get exciting. On the dance floor Timmy Coyle, one of the young slicks from Monte, had his eye on Jeanne and decided the time was right to move in on Warren. "Don't be too hasty to break this up," he told himself as he watched the drama unfold.

Warren and Jeanne had danced most of the evening. From time to time they would change partners on the small dance floor, but in time they always returned to each other. So casually were the social mores practiced here that an outsider might not have recognized the established pairing of couples in the room.

To Timmy Coyle's untrained, or unwilling, urban eyes all women at Buster's were fair game. It was the same standard he practiced at the Eagles Hall, the Armory, and wherever else the rutting urge brought him. To Timmy, women were only and always fair sexual game and he recognized no man's territorial rights.

In the case of Jeanne, his ego did not even take into consideration the acknowledged pairing of her and Warren, and somehow he had all but forgotten his recent and unfortunate encounter with Warren. When Timmy's biological clock called for sex, he unconsciously began to gather his harem, which tonight he perceived to be Jeanne. Like other primitive beasts, Timmy knew he was the alpha male in this crowd and expected only cursory resistance or interference from the other less dominant suitors. This, of course, included Warren, and so it was that Timmy moved to the dance floor.

At Buster's, as it was at most rural social gatherings, courtesy dictated the relinquishing of a dance partner at the tap on the shoulder, the "May I cut in?" and Warren at first responded with the proper courtesy in spite of his feelings toward Timmy. However, by the fourth intrusion into his and Jeanne's private dream world, Warren was no longer amicable. "Thank you, Timmy, but Jeanne and I will finish this dance." They hardly missed a rhythmic step.

Timmy persisted, applying a tight grip to Warren's shoulder. "You misunderstand, Asshole. I'm cutting in." His eyes held a threat as he attempted to turn Warren away.

"Now, listen..." Jeanne snapped, not at all the acquiescent doe she was expected to be. "Why don't you just leave..." Her denial to Timmy was cut short when Timmy turned his back to her, pushing Warren off balance and to the floor.

At first the remaining dancers had not understood the passion play taking place in their midst and continued dancing until they were brought up short by the sparring men. Then, as they recognized the two men they stopped dancing and moved aside.

At the end of the bar Carl smiled. With his back to the dance floor he feigned ignorance of the activity only steps away. After all, as the sheriff, if he had seen the disturbance he might be obliged to bring it to an end. As he watched through the bar mirror, however, he saw something that did get his attention.

As Timmy spun Warren backward, Jeanne had also been thrown off balance. Bumping into another couple as she spun, she sprawled to the floor. At the prospect of a face-off between Warren and Timmy people began clearing the floor, and this left a clear line of sight from Carl's mirror view directly to Jeanne who was now trying in vain to get to her feet. From his vantage point at the bar, Carl was looking directly up Jeanne's skirt, hiked nearly to her hips. Carl's eyes tracked hungrily along her trim legs, following as the pale skin disappeared into the shadowy vagueness beneath her skirt.

In a moment Carl was on his feet, moving, not toward the two men pacing each other in the center of the room, but towards Jeanne. Like a Merino buck weaving through his flock toward an ewe in estrous, he moved. Crossing toward the waiting doe, his upper lip curled almost to his nose as he made his way; not just walking now, but prancing, his intense brown eyes never leaving her, placing each foot surely as he moved quickly toward her, his chest expanded and he quivered all over as his lungs filled with the aroma of her willingness for him and fine beads of perspiration began to cover his lip as he crossed toward her. As he moved his great leathery balls swung surely between his legs.

On the dance floor the action moved quickly. The two antagonists had been quickly separated, not by Timmy's friends who would relish seeing their good friend pop this farmer a time or two, but by Sig Engebretson who had sped to the center of the fray without a moment's thought, and twins Paul and Peter Jenson, who had been sitting with their wives in a nearby booth.

Sig soothed Warren, pulling him into a booth, while the Jensons manhandled Timmy to the other side of the crowded room. After a few heated words Timmy shook loose, heading for the door. As his friends began to catch up with him, Timmy swore to them. Snapping like a chained dog he pushed them away. "Get the hell away from me! I'm just going outside to take a piss. This isn't over yet."

But it was over. Before Timmy returned, before Carl had reached Jeanne's side, the crowd had closed and Warren and Jeanne were pressed together in the booth with the Jensons, and the room returned to normal.

All that remained for Carl was to bawl at Warren for the commotion he caused, threatening to haul him in if there were any more problems. Carl's vision of himself and Jeanne together had once more disappeared.

The little Ford's heater was roaring now as he nursed the Ford onto the highway. The hot air from the heater flashing up to clear the windshield filled the car with its sound. There was not enough heat, however, to keep the side windows clear. The -20 degree temperature combined with the high wind was too intense for the Ford's heat system. "A miserable night," thought Carl as he continued along in second gear. The wind was whipping snow across the road and howling through the night. "A much better night to be home curled up with somebody keeping me warm."

And, indeed, Carl might have gotten to Monte in time to find his little waitress-friend who would help him stay warm through the night, but a few moments later as he passed along the grove of Howard Carlson's farm he saw ahead of him, barely visible in the drifting snow a flutter of black fabric in the snow covered roadway.

A moment later and the hard cold tires of Carl's car would also have run over Ernie's body. It was more curiosity than concern which caused Carl to stop rather than drive past the black flutter in the snow, curious what might have been away, out on a night like this, which had so little traffic. As the Ford crunched to a stop Carl leaped out, leaving the door ajar and the headlights shining at the high drift just ahead of him. Snow from the drifts seeped into his shoes as he pranced lightly to the drift ahead.

Damn! Now my fucking socks will be wet. I'll probably catch my death of cold out here. What a thankless damn job this is! He grabbed at the black fabric, thinking perhaps it was a mitten or a scarf. He had intended to snap it out of the snow and return as rapidly as possible to the warmth of his car, but the cloth he grabbed was a coat sleeve. The heavy snow covering the body snapped Carl back, almost throwing him to his knees. "Son of a bitch!" he cursed aloud. "I should have left the damn thing there." As he turned he saw the cloth in his hand had become a sleeve. The black sleeve encircled a cold white gloveless hand that seemed to be beckoning for Carl's help.

Leaning over, brushing the snow further away, the wind howling and obscuring his vision he soon found the frozen white face. Ernie's mouth was open, his face crusted with ice as he screamed in silent anguish and the lifeless eyes in the frozen white face stared up at Carl.

"Yes," Carl recalled later as he sat at his desk nursing his coffee, "that was one miserable damn night." He had more than wet socks before the night was over.

He had quickly put out flares so some damn farmer wouldn't plow right into his Ford, then with the headlights left on, the gumdrop on top of the car rotating, he trudged up to the nearby farmhouse. After several minutes of banging on the door and yelling, he finally managed to rouse all the sleeping occupants of the house.

While not every farm in Chippewa County had a telephone in 1938, the Carlson's who farmed over three hundred acres of rich farmland, had become one of the earliest participants of the new Bell telephone system. After providing the Carlson's with a sketchy account of his find, Carl turned to use the phone.

Turning the crank on the wall mounted phone while holding the ear cone to his cold wet head Carl yelled at the operator. "Connect me to the goddamn Sheriff's office in Montevideo!" Carl was in no mood to make small talk with the operator who seemed to think she needed to explain that it was storming.

"Send out an ambulance, Kenny," he yelled at his deputy. "No need to hurry, because this poor bastard is dead, but I want you to get out here along with the ambulance." The sleepy Carlsons could not hear the deputy's response but understood when the sheriff continued. "Hell yes, you stupid son of a bitch! I now it's storming! Where do you think I'm calling from, Florida? Jesus! I've got work to do out here, and it's going to be a long night so get your ass moving." He hollered once more into the phone. "Yes, call out the plow if you have to; just get here." Turning then, he thanked the Carlsons, suggesting they put on a big pot of coffee if they might be so inclined, since there were going to be a lot of folks around here before the night was over.

Then, Carl recalled, he had trudged back through the grove and began clearing more snow away from the as yet unidentified body.

CHAPTER

TWENTY-TWO
February 12, 1938

If a mouse is going to try to scare an elephant he needs one of two things: He needs an ace up his sleeve or a quick escape route. Unfortunately, Timmy Coyle had never heard this homily and had neither an ace up his sleeve nor an escape route when he confronted Oliver Martin.

It was payday Saturday at the WPA camp, two weeks to the day after the unfortunate demise of Ernie Hall. It was a night Ollie Martin was planning to celebrate. He was going to get drunk, get laid, and get back to his barracks only when completely satiated.

Timmy was still smarting from his missed opportunity at Buster's, when Warren was saved from what Timmy saw as a sure ass kicking by the untimely arrival of Sig Engebretson. It was beginning to seem that damn Warren led a charmed life, but Timmy knew he could very well be holding an important key to Warren's future.

When Timmy spotted Ollie Martin late in the evening, Ollie was several hours into achieving his first goal and weaving his way down the alley between Andy's Tavern and The Tap. Both taverns had entrances to the alley behind First Street. No one will ever know what Timmy expected to achieve when he confronted Ollie in the dark street. Whatever form of extortion he had in mind, it was Timmy's intention or perhaps just his overgrown ego wanting to make Ollie squirm a bit, the result for Timmy became irrevocable.

"Ollie...Ollie Martin!" Timmy yelled. "You and I need to talk." Ollie was standing shadowed in the alley.

At first Ollie ignored him, but finally responded to the younger man's persistent bark. "Beat it, kid," Ollie responded belligerently. Even if this was Herman's kid, Ollie was in no mood to pamper and coddle the spoiled little asshole. "I got things to do and it's too damn cold for me to stand out here and jaw with you. We've got nothing in common."

"Ah, but we do." Timmy's toothy smile was at its political best. "It seems you and I share a secret and I thought we should talk about it." Timmy's face reminded Ollie how much he hated rich people, thinking they can always get what they want by either kissing your ass or threatening you. He felt his good natured glow slipping away.

Ollie pulled his coat tighter around his neck and leaned further into the shadows. "Now, what do you suppose he's got up his sleeve?"

Timmy quickly covered the space to where Ollie stood in the shadow out of the wind. "I just happen to share some information about one of the men out at the Lac Qui Parle Dam, the one whose body the sheriff found last Saturday. I thought you and I should talk about it for a bit."

"Shit, kid, the sheriff's got that farm kid locked up for that already. Everybody in the county knows he's going up the river for running over old Ernie."

Timmy continued. "It would sure be easy to just let that smart-ass farm boy go in the tank, Ollie, but I thought you might want to make it worthwhile for me to be sure I kept my little secret to myself."

"I don't know what the hell you think you're talking about, kid. You know, it seems to me you damn city boys have always got some game going on. If you got something on your mind spill it. I got to get on down to The Tap."

"Well, Mister Martin," he put special emphasis on the Mister. "I think you'll want to hear what my little secret is," Timmy whispered coyly. "You see, Ollie, a couple of Saturdays ago I was up at Buster's. You remember the night, the Saturday the big blizzard started. You probably saw the way I handled that son of a bitch, Warren out on the dance floor. I'm sure you remember the night. The snow got asshole deep to a tall Indian that weekend; you remember that. You see, after Warren and I got into it, when that damn Engebretson stepped in, I just stepped outside to go to the John."

"I was coming back from the outhouse just east of the place when Ernie Hall left. 'Heading for Watson, I heard him say to one of his pals as he left. He wanted to get where the air was a little clearer. I suspected he was talking about you, since we all know how you two didn't hit it off. Yep, Ernie was heading for a nice quiet beer in Watson. As hard as it was storming I thought the idea wasn't too smart, but then I don't have to live in that barracks all week. I stood and watched as he crossed the ditch there, wading through the snow, and started up the grade on the south side, trying to stay out of the wind. It was a miserable night for walking."

"Then, strangely enough, just about the time I was going to start back into Buster's, I saw you slip your coat on, Ollie. I was standing in the shadows, not on purpose, mind you, but I just happened to be there when you came out."

"Timmy my boy, you've got a pretty good imagination all right. But why would you want to bring me into something like this? I never done you no harm. Besides, I know you and Warren have been strutting around in each other's life like a couple of cock roosters outside a hen house for a long time. Matter of fact, ain't I right that you and him just had words, had another hassle over that little gal friend of his, Jeanne." Ollie smiled as he watched Timmy's face darken with anger. "It seems to me you're just trying to start some trouble here to soothe your own mind for the mental beating that kid gave ya."

"You didn't tell anybody goodbye that I remember Ollie, just eased out like you too were heading for the john. But when you came down the steps you didn't turn my way to the john but went over by the two old cars Buster had parked at the end of the building. I saw you pick up a piece of a car bumper, from a Model A, I think it was. Then I saw you shuffle off into the snow holding it close to your side. It looked to me you were just following right in poor Ernie's foot tracks."

"God! What a night! Remember? A man couldn't see ten feet in front of him. Maybe a man couldn't see ten feet behind him either, especially if he weren't looking for someone to be following him."

"Now, I don't know what happened after you went off into the snow, but it wasn't much later I found out Ernie was dead. Oh, sure, the sheriff is convinced it was our friend Warren, but I'm wondering if that was really the case. It seems a little bit too convenient to me. Yeah, I suppose we can let our friend Warren take a dive for it. What do you think about that Ollie?"

"Now, I'm a peace loving man, Timmy; you know that. All I want is to put in my week's work, have a drink or two on Saturday, get laid once in a while, and get through this miserable winter. I don't think you and I need to get into something over this"

"Ollie, you're right. It seems to me it's only right that Warren should go in the can, make your life and mine simpler. It seems like every time I turn around Warren's stepping on my toes, and as long as he's around it looks like I'm never going to have a chance with Jeanne. I don't know what she sees in that skinny farm bastard, but she just can't keep her eyes off him. One of these days though, if he ends up not going to jail, I'm just going to set his clock cuckoo. And it sure looks like that's where he's going. Carl Brown is determined to get rid of that boy; he just can't stand those farm kids."

"But I'm guessing that if I were to tell the sheriff my story he'd at least want to talk to you. But I'd just as soon see that son of a bitch off to jail and out of here, so why don't you and me talk about how to make Timmy Coyle a happy boy?"

As the young man continued speaking Ollie Martin's mind was racing. He could see Timmy's reason for stopping him in the alley was not just for idle talk, and that he was going to be difficult to deal with. "You can't give in one time to these fellows," he thought. I don't know what he wants, but one thing is going to lead to another. I'll just have to resolve this once and for all, right now."

"Well, maybe you and I do have something to talk about, Coyle." Ollie shirked deeper into his coat and retreated further into the shadows, away from the wind howling around the corner. "I was sure no one saw me leave Buster's. You see, Ernie and I have been sparring for a long time, ever since he beat me out of the teamster's job. I should have had that job, should have kept it, even after Ernie's wounds were healed. Everybody out there knows I'm a better man than Ernie is—ha!—Was, that is," he chuckled. "But I could see it was going to be the same way all winter and all next summer, and until this project is done."

"I finally just had enough of that old boy; you know? And you're right; I followed right in his tracks, paced him right up the hill. That damn wind was howling and the snow was blowing like a son of a bitch, but he was going to town. I think he's been hen housing one of those little gals in Watson once in a while if you ask me. I suspect he was thinking of that as much as a cold beer at Arnie's."

"You know, he didn't even suspect I was behind him till the last minute when I called his name. "Ernie!" I yelled. "Surprise! I said. And when he turned around, heh, heh, heh, he didn't even have time to get his hands up. That piece of cold steel caught him right alongside of the head; I pole axed that son of a bitch. When I was following him I kept thinking how good it was going to be to beat that son of a bitch, to hear him scream for mercy, but he went right to his knees the first time I hit him. I was a little disappointed, but the way he went down I decided once was enough; I just left him lying there."

"You know he must have crawled from the shoulder of the road, come to a little for a minute or two before he passed out." In fact, Ernie was dead when he fell to the snow, the heavy steel from the car bumper had snuffed his life the moment it crushed into his temple.

"It worked out pretty good for me when Warren and his gal friend come driving by a little later and drove over him. It is too bad he's going to go into the can, but I guess if not for that it would have been for something else. Recently I got the impression he's been heading down a bad trail."

Once or twice as they stood in the shadows talking Ollie had dug into his shirt and brought out a Lucky Strike. He'd dug deep into his pants for matches, then hunched his back to the wind and drew life into his cigarette. Now when he reached into his coat Timmy didn't give it a second thought.

This time however, instead of reaching for a cigarette, Ollie's hand went to the long pocket sewn into his mackinaw and the piece of steel bumper nestled there. It had come in pretty handy when he trailed Ernie, so when he'd settled by the wood stove a few nights later he stitched in a piece of denim jeans to the inside of his heavy coat. It worked just like a holster, a nice long sheath he hardly felt just under his arm. The piece of cold steel gave him a sense of added security. "A man never knows when he might have to protect himself," he thought.

Now again he hunched over as if reaching for his cigarettes and turned his side toward Timmy Coyle. Then, fast as an uncoiling spring, he unsheathed the heavy steel, swinging it at arm's length he smashed a glancing blow into the side of Timmy's face, and Ollie heard the young man's jaw break. Planting both feet solid he swung again. This time ribs cracked. Timmy drew in a deep breath as if to scream, his eyes wild with shock and pain, but he was unable to make his voice work. Once again Ollie swung the bar, this time across Timmy's face and the cartilage of his nose collapsed, the flesh turning immediately red and pulpy.

Timmy hurtled back, staggering into the trash cans; he careened into the wall, raising both hands in front of himself. Too frightened and in too much pain to scream now he held his hands out as if fending off a demon spirit.

With a vicious smile on his face Ollie stepped in. "Gosh, I'm sorry Mister Coyle." He couldn't help mimicking Timmy's earlier sarcastic Mister. "I thought sure this was something that would please you, Timmy. After all, you didn't say just what you wanted me to do. And I know how you like flattening out somebody's nose. How do you like THIS?" Again, he swung the flat steel, striking this time solidly against Timmy's arm.

Timmy's left arm went limp, with the bones crushed his arm folded like a towel and he cowered against the wall. Again and again Ollie swung the steel bar. The sound of breaking bones was just barely perceptible over the howling wind, and with each blow Ollie smiled.

As Timmy slowly began to collapse Ollie swung once more, now an overhand logger's chop came across the top of Timmy's head. With a sickening crunch the bone fragments drove deep into Timmy's brain. Timmy's eyes rolled back into his head and with his mouth still open he slid lifelessly into the snow.

Casually now, Ollie dropped the steel bar at Timmy's feet as he looked up and down the alley. *No witnesses, no fingerprints, no sweat. It seems to me, there's no way I can be connected to this.*

Down the alley into the darkness Ollie Martin walked, and as he walked he reached again for his

Luckies. Again he hunched into the wind, with the match bent in the book, he lit the cigarette, then, blowing out the flame, he then dropped the spent match and book into the snow as he disappeared into the night.

CHAPTER

TWENTY-THREE
February 21, 1938

Carl was leaning back in his chair. It seemed as if his feet locked him firmly to the desk in front of him, held him in this, his favorite position. Gesturing wildly and laughing as he recalled each movement, he regaled his deputy with his escapades of the previous night.

"Kenny, you've never seen two more surprised bastards in your life than those young bucks last night. I don't know who they thought they were to come at me like that, but I gave them something to think about, that's for sure. That one poor son of a bitch is sure to have a couple of broken ribs. I don't think they'll get in my way again."

Sometimes when the sheriff talked this way Kenny felt nervous. He wasn't able to clearly identify his feelings, but felt they fell somewhere between embarrassed and ashamed, and he knew better than to interrupt the sheriff with such negative comments.

"Those damn Indians, Kenny. I swear what we ought to do is put the fucking Indians, farmers, and the transients in one big hole and fill that son of a bitch in. This world would be a lot better off if we could just get rid of them. If it weren't for them we'd have a pretty good life out here."

"Of course, them squaws; we could keep them around. What's the latest on our boy Warren? Do we have a court date set? Has anybody said anything about his condition? I didn't like the way that dead teamster's brother looked at me when he came out of Warren's cell the other day. I think we want to get that fellow out of town as fast as we can."

"Sheriff," responded the young deputy with a worried frown, "I forgot to tell you; that Tom Hall fella was in earlier today, before you got in. He asked to see Warren again. I didn't think nothing of it, so I let him in. He was in there about fifteen minutes. When he came out he was mad as hell. I don't know where he was off to, but he sure didn't seem very civil. I'm sorry I forgot to tell you when you first came in. Did I do something wrong by letting him in?"

"Son of a bitch!" Carl's face was livid as he jumped up from his chair, sending it careening across the room. "I don't want anyone in to see Warren after this! If anybody comes in to see him or ask about him I want you to send them in to see me. I don't give a damn who it is. Do you understand? That damn farmer is gonna go in the can, and I don't want anybody to stand in the way. He's responsible for two deaths, and if we're going to have interference from some do-gooder from back east who thinks he's smarter than we are, well we're not gonna have any of that. Now, don't you let anybody in there. I don't give a damn who they are or what they want."

In the span of a single breath Carl's mood seemed to change. "Now get your ass out of here." Once again his cherubic smile creased his face. "I want you to go down to the Bungalow and get me some hamburgers for lunch."

After the deputy left Carl sat hunched over his desk, staring at his empty coffee mug. As he sat alone now, Carl's true mood became more and more ugly. "Son of a bitch." He thought. "Son of goddamn bitch! Stupid, goddamn deputy! Son of a goddamn bitch! Now what does that damn Tom Hall want? What did Warren tell him?"

Grabbing the keys to the jail cell the sheriff stormed down the hall. Standing in front of Warren's cell he glowered through the bars at Warren. Carl's whole body shook with anger. "What in the hell are you trying to stir up?" he yelled at the young prisoner. "You, my friend are going in the can. You're going to go away forever, I'm going to see to that," he yelled again. "I've got you where I want you, Pal. I've got all the evidence I need to put you away," he lied.

"If only I had some more real concrete evidence to tie this son of a bitch to Timmy's death," the sheriff mused aloud. "Even if he didn't do it; I want this boy out of the way. If I could only find some way to tie him to young Coyle's murder. Any evidence at all and no one would believe Jeanne's testimony that they went out to Wegdahl after the confrontation with Timmy. No one would believe that Warren was innocent. Who could be more guilty than Warren, anyway? Who had been fighting with Timmy Coyle for a month, egged on by Timmy Coyle every time he came to town? Who had been antagonized by Timmy Coyle every time he and Jeanne went to Buster's, or the Eagle's, or anywhere for that matter? It would just make sense to everyone that it was Warren who killed Timmy Coyle; if I could only find some concrete way to lay the guilt on him."

"Sheriff," Warren responded weakly from his bunk, "you know as well as I that I didn't kill Timmy Coyle, and you know I wasn't responsible for the death of Ernie Hall. I don't know why you're doing this to me, but we're going to find some way to prove I'm not guilty."

In a rage Carl grabbed the cell bar. His knuckles turned white as he stood staring at Warren for a long minute. Then, smiling, he calmly stepped back. Turning over his shoulder as he passed through door he smiled. "You get a good night's sleep, Warren. We'll see about this." Then he slammed the steel door, and Warren listened as the key grated in the lock. "I wonder what he's up to now," thought Warren as he lay limply on his bunk.

CHAPTER

TWENTY-FOUR
February 21, 1938

Carl was fuming. In agitation he alternated between sitting at his desk clenching, unclenching his fists, and jumping up to storm around the office. "Goddamn that nosy son of a bitch!" He would give anything to know what Tom Hall was up to.

Although his two deputies had seen Carl upset before, in the last year neither had seen him so violent. Both men found duties to perform outside the jail, not wishing to chance being within Carl's reach if he really decided to let go.

When the two men came through the street door sometime later, a gust of wind slammed it hard behind them. "Goddamn it Kenny," Carl yelled, how "how many times do I..." His tirade came to a halt, as, turning, he saw not his deputies, but Tom Hall and Doctor Sam Wilson. "Just wha..." Carl started to yell before he caught himself. "Gentlemen, what can I do for you this afternoon? Mister Hall, you seem to be spending an awful lot of time here, do you like my jail that much?"

"Carl, I understand you have a prisoner who might need some medical attention. Mister Hall here asked me to have a look at him."

"I think Mister Hall is getting awful worried about the well-being of somebody that killed his brother. I don't think you have to worry about my prisoner doc; I'm taking care of him all right."

"I think we should have a look, Carl. Mister Hall thinks he might not live long enough to go to trial unless I do."

Carl could hear the wind roaring deep inside his head. Like a tornado, twisting and uprooting everything in its path the wind blew, darkening everything in his sight. It took all his concentration now as he smiled at Tom and the doctor. "You know, now that you mention it, when I saw him a while back he did look a little sickly, Doc."

"I personally wouldn't care what happens to him, a killer like that. But I suppose we at least need to keep him alive long enough to send to prison."

Tom during this time was keeping a low profile, letting the doctor direct the conversation. As he watched Carl now he tried to understand how this man, who was responsible for maintaining order in the community, could ignore the health of his prisoner this way. The man he saw before him did not fit Tom's understanding of what a protector of the law should be.

"Sheriff," Tom interrupted now, "I got worried when I came in to talk to your prisoner earlier today. He looked pretty sick to me. I didn't know if a doctor had seen him since you arrested him, and although I don't want to stick my nose where it doesn't belong, I thought someone should look at him, just in case." Most of what Tom, said was true. Although Tom thought Warren needed medical attention he knew Warren had not been visited by a doctor since his arrest and beating. Even if he had been certain of Warren's guilt he wasn't sure he could have turned his back on him.

Barely able to control his anger Carl snapped at Tom. "Did you have something special you wanted to see him about, or were you just looking for entertainment? I don't appreciate strangers coming and going in my jail, Mister Hall. I told you I have this case under control. From now on I'd just as soon you butt out of this. Take your brother's body, get on the train, and get the hell out of here. Leave the trial to us."

"Right now, Carl, let's just go have a look at your prisoner." Doc Wilson now started for the cell block door, leaving little opportunity for Carl to argue. "We don't want to interfere, Carl," he placated. "But I am responsible for the wellbeing of your prisoners."

As the trio made their way along the hall toward Warren's cell Carl had time to collect himself. "What in the hell was I thinking of? Keep cool, Carl, cool. You're still going to have Warren in the can."

From behind the steel door, the sounds of labored coughing and stifled cries reached the three men. When the cell door was thrown open, Tom's fears were realized. Warren was lying on the bed coughing; with every cough pale blood bubbled from his mouth. In pain, frightened by his inability to help himself or call out for help, he whimpered, oblivious of the men outside.

"Carl, call an ambulance. This man is going to the hospital right now; at least he is if he lives long enough to move him." In the first seconds Doc Wilson recognized the symptoms of a punctured lung. "Lucky, if that's all that's wrong," he thought as he looked at Warren's pale gray face. "Hustle, Carl. This man's life might depend on it." The doctor actually believed that Carl cared.

"Tom, help me turn him a little, but be careful of his chest there. He sure doesn't look good; I don't know why the sheriff didn't have me look at him before."

Tom was wondering the same thing. When he had been in to see Warren earlier in the day, his condition had not been nearly so serious. He had seen Warren convulse in pain when he coughed, but at that time the prisoner seemed stable, if breathing irregularly. Warren had been able to respond to the questions Tom posed. As Tom left the cell block a spasm of coughing had sent Warren to the bunk in pain. Tom spotted a fine line of brightly colored blood at the corner of Warren's mouth and knew for sure then that the young man was in trouble.

"I only hope I didn't take too long finding Doc Wilson," Tom thought now as they worked to make Warren ready as possible to move. "I'm a little worried. What do you think, Doc?"

"I won't know until I get him into the hospital, but he's in serious trouble. Thank God you convinced me to come with you."

CHAPTER

TWENTY-FIVE
February 26, 1938

"Christ, what a week." Carl was starting to feel like a dog chasing his tail. He still hadn't gotten over the insult of Tom Hall bringing Doc Wilson into the jail and having his prisoner taken to the hospital. He was also disappointed in his lack of self-control, letting his emotions get the best of him when Hall showed up with the doctor. If Carl knew anything, Carl knew how to project the right image at the right time. He couldn't remember the last time he had lost control like that.

It looked like Warren was going to survive, although it had been touch and go for a couple of days with the punctured lung. By the time Warren was admitted to the hospital, he had a fever that almost killed him by itself, but Doc had finally saved him. "Too bad; my problems would have been over if the son of a bitch had just died." When the ambulance took Warren away Carl had stood smiling from his window. "What better way," he thought, "to solve both the hit and run and Timmy Coyle's murder. Dead men don't argue." Never mind that so far he hadn't been able to find the evidence he needed to pin the Coyle murder on Warren; it would only be a matter of time. But with him dead, Carl's innuendoes would suffice. "Guilty."

Now, with Warren settled in the hospital, Carl guided his Ford toward the transient camp. He was trying to decide how to deal with the upcoming encounter with

Ollie Martin. Over the past weeks' time, Carl had heard rumors, indirectly passed, and whispered in the bars that the night of his death Ollie had been seen with Timmy.

Ollie had taken over Ernie Hall's team of horses after Hall's death, and there was just a chance the rumors were coming from someone who thought he should have the teamster job instead of Ollie. But Carl thought he should check the story out, to protect himself if nothing else.

Carl had planned to get out to the camp earlier in the week, Thursday morning. However, he had a frantic call from Herman Coyle. Herman hadn't wanted to call the police chief he said, didn't want to bother him, but Herman's wife Emma was missing and he was worried. "Didn't want the embarrassment, more likely," Carl thought. "But he doesn't mind interrupting me, as if I have nothing better to do than look for Herman's goddamn wife."

Carl had almost told Herman the way he treated his wife he wouldn't be surprised if she had run off to Minneapolis or someplace with one of Herman's clothing salesmen, screwing her brains out." But under the circumstances, having just buried Timmy less than a week ago, Carl held his piece. "Someday, though, I'd like to have a closer look at her ass," Carl thought. "Not bad for an old broad!"

Since Timmy's death Emma's world had changed. The thin line between reality and fantasy had blurred and then disappeared altogether. Emma seemed to be living in a dream. Now, in her dream world, the sound of the violins filled the air; soft, light strains that seemed to glide like thin clouds down through the trees, drifting lightly and melodiously around her, giving Emma such a wonderful feeling of grace and freedom. When she and

Herman danced like this Emma was at peace with the world.

Somewhere she could hear water falling, humming in tune with the violins. She couldn't see the water. She thought it was probably coming from the tall marble fountain beyond those trees over there to her right, a tall fountain with laughing cherubs dancing lightly in the spray and foam. The cool water was falling from tier to tier, filling the air with a delicate mist which whispered so softly to her in the night. In the depths of the fountain's pool there were exotic koi; white, black, mottled orange giants gracefully twisting and gliding among the lovely marble children, rubbing against their legs while they cavorted there as if time stood still.

It was such a lovely night. "Oh, Darling," she whispered dreamily. "I just want to dance forever." Herman was holding her in his strong arms, guiding her in great lyrical orbits among the park's huge sentinel oaks, protecting her as he guided her, keeping her safe from the mysteries lurking in the night.

Emma could hear the piano, a huge black concert grand, accompanying the violins, now lightly filling the air like summer breezes gently tinkling through the huge chandelier, then at times heavy and somber, deep base notes almost below the range of her hearing, like thunder, rumbling out there in some dark cavern. All the beautiful shiny instruments were playing just for her and Herman. She must remember to thank everyone for coming.

Today she felt so elegant, so beautiful; no wonder Herman loved her so. "Emma, I'll love you the rest of my life. Nothing will ever come between us." She laughed when she heard him whisper. In his eyes Emma could see her reflection as they danced on and on. Her cheeks were rosy, flushed from the excitement and the cold, accenting the delicate line of her soft full lips. Her hair was in great loose coils falling behind her ears. Herman loved her ears, nibbled them gently as he whispered naughty things which made her laugh. Her rich brown mane floated behind as they whirled around and around, sweeping all their cares away.

Emma was wearing no makeup tonight but she knew she looked ravishing as she gazed back at Herman. Around her neck was a black rope of woven silk and suspended by a silver thread so delicately beneath it, a single perfect pearl.

When the dancing started the sky had been cloudy, cold, and stormy threatening to spoil the dance, ruin her gown, and the wind gave her a chill, sending shivers al through her. But now the shadows lengthened, and the moon had taken charge once again, driving away the clouds and the breeze was just lightly caressing her as she danced. By moonlight, with a million stars flickering above them they danced. The light reflected from the glistening snow was so bright, a spotlight which followed them in their dance of love; Emma felt so fulfilled.

As they drifted among the trees now Emma glanced at her lovely gown flowing about her. Gently brushing the snow covered ground at her feet, the gown billowed over her long full slips before clinging to her hips. At her waist, the satiny gown gathered, and gently encircled her sensuously curving stomach, her ample breasts proudly filled the bodice, trimmed in the finest lace, delicately accenting her soft pale skin.

Somewhere far off in the trees she could her name called, "Emma…Emma…," such a sad sound she didn't answer, just kept on dancing. It was so far off, "on top of that hill, perhaps," she thought. "I'll just keep on dancing until they all go away, dancing in my lovely black gown, …so black, so lovely…"   Carl hadn't really expected to find Emma. He came only to pacify Herman. "Someday I might need a favor and it'll be nice to have the old bastard owe me a favor." At first Carl had followed Herman around the big ugly house, listening to him whine about how unappreciated all his hard work was, and brag about all the ugly furnishings, explaining in detail the origin of each piece.

"God all mighty," Carl thought as he followed Herman from room to room. "Am I here to learn how his old lady spends his money, or to find out where she ran off to?" Finally, they ended their tour standing in front of Emma's nightstand.

"She hasn't been the same since Timmy's funeral, Carl. All she does is walk back and forth between this room and the bay window."

"Where do you think she might have gone? Maybe she's just at one of the neighbors, or one of her friends from your country club." Carl couldn't see anything indicating foul play, so he figured Herman was just upset that she hadn't told him she was going out.

"Carl, she wouldn't have gone to any of the neighbors, and she sure as hell wouldn't have anything to do with women from the club. She can hardly stand them, only goes with me to make me happy. But where could she have gone? Christ! I'm worried about her."

As they looked through Emma's things Carl noticed a couple of items missing, asked Herman where they might be. "I don't pay any attention to that stuff, Carl. I've got enough on my mind just keeping the store going. Hell, if supper weren't on the table, I wouldn't know where to look for something to eat."

After searching the home's attic and basement they circled the outside of the house, seeking some clue as to Emma's activities. As he was about to give up and turn back to the driveway Carl noticed something in the snow beneath a low hanging bush at the edge of the yard. He called Herman as he retrieved a small oval framed picture nearly covered with snow. "Oh, God," Herman moaned. "That's a picture of Timmy when he was little. What do you think it's doing out here?"

"My guess is that she dropped it as she walked down this path, Herman. Have you ever seen her come out here?"

"Oh…sure. Sometimes she walks out there to the edge of the hill and watches the young people down on the lagoon. But why would she come out here now? I know in the summer she watches everything that goes on down in the park, Carl. Sometimes she stands out here for hours, it seems, in the bay window up there." He pointed back to the house, and the window which overlooked the park and the valley.

"Do you two ever walk down there, by the park I mean? An idea was starting to form. Carl frowned, studied Herman as he guided him back toward the house.

If there was going to be a problem down there, Carl decided, he sure didn't want Herman following him around.

"In the summer sometimes Emma and I used to walk in the park. That was before the city even turned it into a park, I guess. When we got married we had our wedding reception in the park. It was something grand, I want to tell you. There used to be a bandstand over there," he motioned across the lagoon. "We hired a band and served champagne, the whole shebang! Emma and I danced half the night, right on the grass. Emma couldn't get enough…just danced and danced until I thought we'd spend the whole night there." He blushed slightly, thinking the sheriff could tell he'd rather have been off in bed with Emma. "I wonder why I haven't thought about it in such a long time."

Leaving Herman at the house Carl worked his way through the trees, following a faint trail down the hill. He crossed the road which eventually became Main Street and crossed into Lagoon Park. From the partially frozen river he heard the sound of the water as it cascaded over the small dam at the edge of the park. Snow blanketed the park and the lagoon which in the summer was such an attraction for swimmers and boaters. For long minutes there was no sign of Emma and Carl began to think she had not come this way after all. Then, as he was about to head back to the house on the hill, his eye caught a flutter of color in the snow.

When Carl first saw her curled up beneath a bush he was certain Emma was dead. A hundred feet earlier he had spotted one of her furry slippers. It had been the absence of slippers and robe in Emma's bedroom which convinced Carl that she had not run off with some man. All her other belongings were in place, jewelry, fur coat, makeup. No woman leaves home without her makeup, Carl knew.

From the bay window on the hill he thought Emma had probably been able to see the place in the park where she and Herman danced, where she had been happy some time far in her past. There was a slight chance she had wandered off, her mind disoriented over the loss of her son.

Now, as he approached Emma, curled in a fetal position in the snow, he wished he had been wrong in guessing where she might be. Carl had followed her trail through the powdery snow for thirty minutes or more, wandering among the trees with no apparent goal. She had crossed and re-crossed her own trail several times. Carl couldn't understand; even here, deep in the woods, she should have been able to find her way home. In the distance he could hear cars as they crossed through the valley. Less than fifty yards away was the riverbank, and not far away was the sound of the river.

The sun filtered through stark branches and cast abstract shadows on Emma's still form as Carl approached. "No hurry," Carl told himself, believing the still figure in the snow was dead. "Thank God, I left Herman at the house. I can imagine trying to get her body out of here with a hysterical husband stumbling all over me." In the snow Emma looked old, pathetic. Although she was not quite fifty her dirty gray hair was matted around her pale face. She wore a flowered chenille robe, one slipper still covering an exposed foot. As Carl kneeled at her side however, his breath caught in his throat. The lifeless eyes staring past him blinked, tried to focus, but could not seem to comprehend his presence. "Jesus Christ!" thought Carl.

In amazement Carl stared for a moment at the woman curled before him. Somehow Emma was alive. Undoubtedly in shock she seemed completely unaware of her circumstances. "Mrs. Coyle, Emma!" Now Carl moved rapidly, knowing with certainty that every moment now could affect Emma's life. Carl removed his heavy coat, wrapping it around her. Emma was unable to assist him, making a simple task more difficult. Carl sensed that if he left her, went to bring assistance, she could well be dead by his return. Kneeling again in the snow Carl lifted Emma, then lurched to his feet and turned toward the roadway in the distance. "Emma, old girl, right now it's a good thing you're twenty pounds overweight. It might just have saved your life." Emma's eyes stared at the sky. Her limp body unaware as sharp branches thrashed her delicate skin as Carl struggled to carry her from the park.

CHAPTER
TWENTY-SIX

Although Carl had been watching for Ollie Martin as he drove from Montevideo, there had been no sign of the transient teamster. Cautiously, he parked his car near the heavy construction equipment lined carefully along the road and began to walk into the quiet camp. If Ollie were not still somewhere in the camp Carl would check across the road at Buster's. He hoped Ollie was still in the camp.

Dusk was overtaking the construction camp. The early winter sunset with its flat winter light cast few shadows through the trees. The partly frozen river murmured beneath the deep bank. Carl shivered; it felt to him then as if there was a sinister aura settling over the darkening camp.

Carl did not like all the changes that were taking place in the area. Building the dam, moving the road, were unnecessary. He would like to see everything stay as it was. There was something unsettling about all the activity here these days; these changes were not necessarily progress to Carl's way of thinking.

As many as three hundred men lived at this camp during the main summer construction season, but it was a much lighter crew that stayed during the winter when much of the construction work was curtailed. Over the last eighteen months Carl had watched the progress as men and horses and heavy equipment changed what had been a quiet wooded valley into a turmoil of construction, and he didn't like it.

Now, when the rain came the hillside was a quagmire, and the river ran thick and muddy brown all the way past the Stay Bridge. Huge tree stumps pushed up from the nude loam along the river's banks, and during the week, even in the depth of winter the air was filled with the roar of huge laboring engines as dirt and rock were removed with no pattern Carl could determine. He doubted the fishing would ever again be good in the river.

A huge dike, nearly two miles long, stretched in a gentle curve across the valley now, and men were covering the dike's slopes with a checkerboard of split granite which would restrict erosion. By now the new road leading directly down the hill, to what by spring would be a huge concrete bridge built atop the new spillway, had been laid.

"Right now, however, the whole damn place looks like a war zone," thought Carl. Concrete bridge and dam forms were set in some places, and stacked haphazardly in others, waiting to be used. Snow and mud mixed in a big checkerboard, some places standing at least knee deep in the dirty ice crusted water. It was no wonder Carl stayed as far from this place as he did.

Walking carefully through the snow, trying to stay on high ground away from the slush caused by the daily traffic of trucks and horses, Carl continued into the darkening camp. He casually asked the only man he saw if Ollie Martin was still around camp. "No need to create more visibility here than necessary," he thought.

"I seen him over in the shower shack not over a half hour ago, but I'm not sure he's still in camp," the man replied as he pointed toward the back row of buildings.

The man left Carl as soon as he had answered, and a few moments later Ollie stepped out of the shower shack. He looked startled at finding the sheriff walking his way. He quickly masked his surprise and his apprehension at seeing the sheriff in camp. In all the while he had worked here neither the sheriff nor his deputies had been on the construction site unless something serious had taken place.

Ollie's eyes quickly scanned the camp. Seeing no one else about, he descended the steps from the shower shack. He thrust his hands in his pockets and casually stepped toward the sheriff and into the nighttime shadows. "You're a long way from home, Sheriff. What brings you down here on a Saturday? Things surely can't be as exciting here as they are over at Buster's. Seems to me I heard your favorite place on a Saturday is hanging on the end of the bar watching all those girls with their cute little asses swinging around there. Of course it's a little early yet, I suppose. I reckon you're just slumming."

"Ollie, Ollie, Ollie," the sheriff intoned with a smile on his face. "You need to be more respectful to me. After all, I am the law around here—regardless of what you might think."

"There it was," thought Carl. "Goddamn transients forget what their place is in this fucking world." Although he appeared casual and relaxed as he spoke to Ollie, with his own hands thrust deep in the pockets of his alpaca coat, collar pulled high around his neck, Carl was by no means casual in his observation of the man before him. You didn't stay Sheriff by taking men like this for granted.

"You stupid son of a bitch," he was thinking. "I really don't give a damn if you killed Timmy Coyle or not right now; but I do know it's time I showed you a lesson in manners."

"Let's just step over here, out of everybody's way, Ollie. We don't want one of those poor assholes coming out here to take a piss and get the hell scared out of him by finding us here in the shadows."

He guided Ollie further into the trees. Walking toward the high bank of the river, Carl stood looking out over the snow covered stream. The river's soft, gray, ice-covered surface was interrupted by occasional dark patches of open water. The entire stretch below camp showed the exposure of open water caused by the heated wastewater from the cook house and shower shack. "This part of the river probably doesn't freeze over all winter," thought Carl.

"Ollie, I got a couple of things I have to ask you. Now, you know there's no love lost between me and you fellows working out here. But I like to stay clear, let you fellows handle your own problems when I can." Carefully Carl watched, tensing slightly as Ollie's hand dipped inside his coat.

Ollie brought out a pack of Luckies and a book of matches. "You don't mind if I smoke, do you Sheriff? Have one? No? Okay." Ollie shook a Lucky Strike out of the pack, plucked it from the pack with his lips, "like a horse lifting the last kernel of corn from the feed box," Carl thought.

Then the sheriff watched as Ollie bent the match, still in the book, zipped the match along the strike surface with his thumb, and cupping his hand in a protective shell drew fire into the cigarette. As he exhaled, Ollie stripped the broken match from the book and dropped it to the ground. In one smooth motion he then put matches and cigarettes back inside his coat.

"Sweet Jesus," thought Carl as he tried to mask his surprise. "That's exactly how those matches looked that I found beside Timmy. You'd better play this a little more careful," he told himself.

"Ollie, I'm trying to do a little checking into where everyone was last Saturday. I had a couple of fellows tell me they thought they saw you talking to young Timmy Coyle the night he was murdered. Can you tell me where you were on Saturday?"

"Why sure, Sheriff. I hitched a ride into Monte with one of the farmers out here Saturday afternoon. I got done early on Saturday, thought maybe I'd get me one of those good hamburgers at the Bungalow, and maybe take in a movie. I heard some of the boys say that new Ronald Coleman movie about the French Foreign Legion was pretty good; Under Two Flags was the name of it, I think."

"But, then after I had the hamburger I got to feeling not too good. Maybe it was too greasy. Then about the time I was trying to decide whether to take in the movie or head out to Watson, I spotted young Timmy Coyle. Like the fellows said, I was talking to him for a while. But I wasn't down the alley. I was just around the corner from the movie house."

"Young Coyle was asking me some questions about the camp. Seems he thought next summer he'd like to get hired on out here, I guess. WPA money's not all bad, you know. Then, we went on our own way. Why shucks, it was pretty early. I sure don't know how anybody could figure I was around there later when young Coyle got himself killed."

"Of course, he'd been drinking a bit already by the time I was talking to him. As I understand, he got into a squabble with that Warren fella. Knowing how Timmy was I suppose he egged him into something and ended up paying the price."

"It doesn't sound to me like you've got much to hide, Ollie. I imagine lots of folks talked to young Coyle on Saturday."

"Oh, by the way," Carl added, "one of the fellows I was talking to said you had a special place sewn into your coat where you kept a weapon of some kind. Mind if I have a look at that?" When Ollie seemed to hesitate, Carl continued. "Consider this an official request, if you will, Ollie."

"Sure thing, Sheriff; I got nothing to hide from ya." His hand went into his coat. Again, out came the cigarettes and matches, and again the folding and striking of the match. All the while stalling for time, Ollie was trying to decide how to handle the sheriff. To open his coat now and to show the sheriff the piece of cold steel he had tucked inside his mackinaw would be tantamount to shouting out his guilt. Since that last piece of cold steel had worked well, Ollie had picked up an almost identical piece from that same scrap pile. It looked now like it might be his downfall unless he thought of something mighty quick.

There was no way to get out of this now unless he might surprise the sheriff. One good swift blow, the sheriff had his hands in his pockets, after all. And he could dump the sheriff into the open water. Down the river he'd go, under the ice. By spring there'd be nothing left even to come to the surface.

Well, let's have it, Martin," the sheriff said.

"Of course, Sheriff," Ollie replied. "My mind was just wandering a bit there. I've got nothing to hide from you." With his left hand he unbuttoned his coat, pulled the front away as if to show the sheriff he had nothing to hide. He looked the sheriff in the eye as his right hand, still holding the cigarettes and matches, went toward his pocket. Then, deftly, the hand dropped few inches to the top of the steel bar.

Like lightening, Ollie drew the steel out and swung at the sheriff. Only at the last instant did Carl realize he had been caught off guard.

Throwing his hand up toward off the powerful blow, Carl rolled with the arc of the steel bar. Even though he was rolling with the blow, pain shot through Carl's arm as the unexpected attack threw him to the ground. On his back, he rolled over in time to see Ollie swing again. Carl lurched to the side in time to save himself, then jammed his feet into Ollie's chest.

Even through the heavy coat Ollie felt a rib crack but continued to press his attack. He threw himself at his opponent, trying to grab him by the neck with his free hand while he tried to hammer Carl with the steel bar.

Carl couldn't believe he had been off guard and for a moment, he almost admitted to himself he had underestimated Ollie. As Ollie charged again Carl lashed out with a foot, catching Ollie on the side of the knee, and Ollie caromed off balance into a large tree where, stunned, he dropped the weapon, sliding to the ground.

With both hands now Carl clawed furiously for his life. Grabbing Ollie's wrist he wrestled him back to the ground. As the two slammed to the ground they rolled into the brush. Then, as if by a miracle, Carl found the piece of bumper within his reach, and grabbing for his life he took the offensive. The cat was out of the bag.

They both knew now who the guilty man was; there would be no stopping. There'd be no walking away. There would be no alibis.

The two men lurched to their knees as the sheriff tried to regain his balance Ollie's toe caught him in the pit of the stomach and he leaped once more onto the sheriff. Carl slammed the heel of his hand into Ollie's nose; the blood gushed and the hot sticky liquid oozed into the sleeve of Carl's coat. Again he slammed Ollie, and then realizing he held the steel bar, Carl swung, but lost his footing and slipped again to the ground, dropping the bar. Again, Ollie charged, but now his endurance was gone and Carl's blows began to take their toll, Ollie's eyes began to lose their focus. Finally, regaining his balance, Carl reached again for the steel bar at his feet. In one long swoop he smashed the bar into Ollie's head. Still, Ollie staggered forward. Another smashing blow, but Ollie continued to charge.

Carl's breath was coming in great ragged gasps, and his legs felt as if they were rubber, incapable of holding him up. As Ollie lurched forward one more time Carl mustered his strength, and with a guttural roar he swung the bar with a backhand blow that stopped Ollie's advance.

With a look of disbelief Ollie slumped to his knees. Blood began to ooze from what remained of his mouth. His surprised expression turned to hate, then at last turned to fear as he crumpled forward, dead in the snow.

It seemed unlikely that any of the hangers-on in the shower shack or the bunkhouses had seen or heard what happened. If such a man existed, he did not come forward. These two men—Carl Brown, and Ollie

Martin—were two of the most feared and hated men in the area. Their discussion, and the brawl ending in Ollie's death, had been hidden from view by the large trees along the river. The river itself, gurgling in the night, muffled many of the grunts, moans, and yells of the brawl.

Kneeling beside Ollie's broken body, Carl dragged in deep ragged breaths of air. His own body was racked with nervous tremors. As he thought now of bringing Ollie's body in and of having solved the murder of Timmy Coyle a slow grin filled his face. Carl leaned back and chuckled. "Well, I'll be damned! If this don't beat all! It seems as if I solved two problems at once here."

"On the one hand I can bring Ollie in, and with the discovery of the second piece of iron in his coat, the matches and cigarettes which match those I found in the alley, we can have this case closed in no time. On the other hand, if Ollie were to disappear I still have a good chance to see Warren convicted of killing Coyle. No more Ollie at the camp, no more Warren to cause trouble every time I see him. I don't see how I can lose."

The longer Carl thought on this idea the more sense it made to him. *How to get rid of the body?* he questioned himself. The gurgling of the river in the background provided the answer to his question. *Of course! Why didn't I think of that right away. It's as obvious as the sweat running down my face. Dump the body in the river. He'll be tumbling along under the ice, no telling how far. His disappearance can be explained, just like all the others, who leave here at the end of a work week. With his paycheck in hand, what better time for a man to seek warmer climates? Of course. And if the body ever does show up down river it'll be easy to explain. He was standing on the riverbank taking a piss and fell in, the heavy winter clothes keeping him from getting out of the water. He's dragged under the ice by the heavy current and that's all there is to it.*

As he looked around Carl saw no one in the camp. Night had now settled firmly along the Minnesota River. Across the highway the sounds of Saturday's revelry were beginning to drift toward him.

"Good riddance, Ollie," he whispered as he dumped the lifeless form over the bank. Bouncing once on the frozen clay before it slid into the river, Ollie's body floated for a few moments while the bulky clothing soaked up the water. Then it slipped slowly out of sight into the dark water. Carl threw the steel bar over the bank after him. "The end of Ollie Martin and the end of Warren," he thought with a smile. "Now I just have to figure how to get a firm conviction for Warren."

Chapter

Twenty-seven

Tom had been in Montevideo for two weeks. He thought the stop here that was going to be painful but simple, just arrange for transportation of Ernie's corpse, and get back to the train, had now entered a new phase. February was gone. With it went the winter's most bitter temperatures, which Tom was very pleased to have missed, thank you, and the heavy snows of the early winter had subsided. Although Tom believed he had seen two weeks of miserable cold, this February had been mild by the standards of the region. On many days, the temperatures had risen into the middle twenties, and frequently stayed above zero overnight as late afternoon winds brought in cloud cover which kept the temperatures from plummeting as they had in the early winter. It had all the earmarks of an early spring, which left the local residents with mixed emotions.

Although the drought which had plagued the prairies for several years was past, an early spring could easily be the forerunner of another year short on moisture, causing more poor corps. People on the streets everywhere were talking about the weather which was so instrumental not only to their physical comfort, but also to their financial well-being.

Warren's trial date was set to begin March sixth, a Monday. The sheriff was still trying to convince everyone of Warren's guilt and the prosecutor said he was expecting a verdict of first degree murder. "Second degree murder isn't even a consideration," Carl had announced, because Timmy's body had been so horribly brutalized." The prosecutor was convinced, as was most of Chippewa County, that Warren, who was frustrated and angered by the continued harassment, had waited for Timmy Coyle, called him into the dark alley, then broke his arms and ribs before finally smashing his skull. Then, in contempt, he dropped the bumper section in the snow and walked away.

Life for everyone in the Minnesota River valley had gone on as usual. Things were very much the same in Boyd and Canby, and in Pinch Town, and in Milan and Watson. Things were also much the same at the Lac Qui Parle Dam construction site, and in the transient camp. Saturday night continued to bring farmers to Buster's, some to play their violins, accordions, and guitars, while others danced or just visited, catching up on the latest country gossip. And the young people continued to drift in for a few drinks of moonshine, cut with Coca Cola to reduce its bite. Some would dance for a while, as in the past, then wander off into the night.

One thing was different, however, because for the past two weeks a stranger, Tom Hall, had been finding his way into people's lives. Tom had visited the taverns in Boyd and Canby and he had been at Buster's on Saturday's. The farmers along the Watson Sag and around the Lac Qui Parle Dam had been visited by this stranger whose brother they had learned to accept, and surprisingly learned to like. In Watson, Tom had was at Arnie's, playing pool, and talking with the men who worked construction when the weather allowed. Day by day Tom Hall had seen those who were friends of his brother; he had also seen some in this rural community who were not friends of Carl Brown.

In the time his brother Ernie had lived and worked in this rural community he had in fact made many friends, and Ernie's friends immediately became Tom's friends. Each day the information he gathered became more interesting, and each day Tom was more certain that an unanswered mystery was still to be solved. The puzzle which at first had been as unreadable as the gray snow drifting across the barren fields was gaining some color and becoming readable.

By now Tom was convinced he knew why Sheriff Brown disliked Warren. Tom had been told, many times, about the way Carl lusted for Jeanne and how Carl sat at the end of the bar, watching as she and Warren danced and cuddled, as young lovers will do. He had also been told ,several times, of Carl's disdain for Warren, how Carl would treat Jeanne. Carl, it seemed, was open and vocal about many things. Then, one afternoon, as Tom was sipping a Coke and talking with Buster, a man silently slipped in to sit at a stool at the far end of the bar.

Buster served the man a Coke. From his heavy coat the newcomer pulled a flask and poured a shot of clear liquor into the bottle. After he returned the flask into the pocket, he sat quietly sipping his drink, staring into the mirror, seemingly unaware of Tom's presence.

After several minutes, the quiet man motioned to Buster, and a furtive conversation took place at the end of the bar, after which Buster returned to face Tom. "That fellow at the end of the bar is one of the cooks over at the camp, wants to talk to you. He's been waiting, he says, for a chance to talk to you when none of the other men were around. Says he has something maybe you'd like to know."

Tom moved to the stool next to the stranger, who cast a furtive glance around the room, then began. "Mister, I work as a cook across the road at the camp. Usually we don't like to get involved with the regular folks here, but I liked your brother; a lot of us here did."

"I think I know something you might like to know, but I don't want to talk to you here. I'm gonna go out the door and go over where all that road building equipment is. You look over there and you'll see a tool shack. Wait a few minutes, then come over if you don't see anybody watching you." Tom watched the man chug-a-lug the rest of his coke, then walked out the door.

As he crossed the road, Tom looked about him, but saw no one. There was still snow on the ground, but rather than the pristine white which had greeted him as he stepped from the train in Montevideo, Tom was greeted by a blanket of dirty gray snow, which hid in the shadows of the trees and heavy equipment and was gone altogether where the sun heated the heavy soil. For several days the wind, announcing that spring was near, had been blowing dirt around the construction site. Even the most recent dusting of snow only nights before had a dirty look about it. The dirt itself trapped the heat of the sun and caused the snow to melt more rapidly than in the woods or even on the open prairies. It would not be many more days before the spring thaws would change the landscape, preparing it for another season of hope.

Tom entered the tool shed, and as his eyes adjusted to the darkness he saw the camp cook leaning back on a rickety cane-back chair. As Tom watched, the man reached in his pocket and retrieved a cotton sack of Bull Durham. From a small sheaf he withdrew a flimsy cigarette paper, then gently shook the tobacco into its center, deftly rolled the paper to settle the tobacco, licked it once and twisted it into a dark heavy smoke. The cook watched Tom intently as he lit his cigarette, then after inhaling several times he began his story.

"Well, you see," he hesitated; then he rushed on as if he needed to tell his story before his nerve left him. "I was in the cook shack last Saturday night, like I usually am. Some of the cooks come in early for the breakfast shift. Me, I come in a little later. Then I stay after everybody else gas gone, to take care of things, clean up and get ready for the next day; you know. I just finished doing up all the kettles. I had everything in line to fix breakfast Sunday morning for those boys that was still around camp and I was planning to head over to Buster's a little later. I usually go over there on Saturdays, not during the week, though. Some of the guys go into town, but I don't feel comfortable there. Anyway, I sort of enjoy some of that music, and sometimes I even play my harmonica with the band if they don't mind. Maybe the music's not as good as Whoopee John, from over in Hutchinson, but he doesn't get to these little places like Buster's. Sometimes he plays in Monte at the Eagle's hall, though."

He blushed at having gotten off his subject, as if he hadn't planned to get so personal. "I was just untying my apron, to hang it on the hook next to the door, when I saw one of the construction crew out there talking to someone."

The little man hesitated, puffed on his hand-rolled cigarette, blowing smoke at the ceiling. "Well, I heard these two fellas talking outside, you see. I was just nosy, I suppose, about who was still around, because on Saturday most of the boys head for town or for Buster's across the road. You probably wouldn't know about it, but paydays don't come often enough when you live in a barracks out in the middle of nowhere."

"Well, as I looked out I saw the sheriff talking with one of the boys who'd just come out of one of the barracks. I saw this fellow turn and point back into the camp a ways and then turn and leave. The sheriff stood and watched him go. As I was about to get my coat I saw him stop, kind of looking around the camp. He looked strange, kind of suspicious, if you know what I mean; like somebody trying to hide rather than looking for another man."

"I watched him as he walked careful-like back into the camp. About this time I saw Ollie Martin step outside. He'd just come from the shower shack, pulling his big coat on as he walked through the door. Then, him and the sheriff walked off towards the river, talking friendly-like. Although I never seen them two together before I didn't see anything unusual about that. A few minutes later, as I was standing there I seen the sheriff come back out of the woods. He looked around, careful-like again, before he came out of the trees. Then, as if he didn't want to be seen, the Sheriff bee-lined it for the road up there. As I watched, I saw he had his car parked up there, by the construction area. I remember thinking then that it was unusual; knowing the kind of man the sheriff is. I figured he'd be the kind who'd just drive right up and not get his feet muddy or anything."

"Well, I didn't think no more about it. Maybe I just didn't want to think about it. I put on my coat and went out and had a few drinks. Well, come Monday, when all the boys were showing up for breakfast, one of the cat operators asked where Ollie was. No one had seen him around. I was just going to say I'd seen him talking to the sheriff on Saturday when I thought better of it; kept it to myself."

The little man looked up from under hooded eyebrows. After a long moment he started again, this time speaking nervously. "When Ollie didn't show up at all on Monday, I got to thinking again about seeing him and the sheriff. Ollie's not the kind of guy you miss, 'cause he kind of bulls his way around, looking for the best cut of meat or looking for the warmest place by the stove. I saw where it looked like two guys stood talking, lots of cigarette butts down there and matches on the ground. Then I saw the snow seemed sort of scuffed up over towards the river. I looked again and saw some blood there."

"I decided I'd better keep my mouth shut. There's plenty of ways a man can get in trouble around here without his going around talking about the sheriff being involved in something at the camp. But if you ask me, I'd say Ollie and the sheriff had some kind of discussion over there. When it was all done Ollie never came back out."

"By now, of course, there's nothing to see over there. We've had some warm days and a couple of snowfalls overnight but, if you want to have a look down there mister I'd suggest you go down past the shower shack. Walk over by where the water drains into the ravine and the ravine drains into the river. I doubt you'll find anything, but you might feel better knowing you've looked for yourself."

"Of course it's just as likely Ollie and the sheriff just had a falling out over some little thing, and when it was all over Ollie just decided it was time to leave this country. Payday is when a lot of the boys decide to leave. Some just get on a train down in the Sag over there by Watson. Some go into Monte where they can catch the

Milwaukee Road train. The way winters are around here I'm surprised anybody sticks it out."

Without further comment the little man tilted his chair back to the floor, walked to the door. Pausing for a moment at the door he looked round the construction site, then slipped out, leaving Tom standing alone in the shack.

CHAPTER

TWENTY-EIGHT

After the camp cook left Tom took his seat in the cane back chair, also leaning back against the wall. As he puzzled at the story he had just been told, Tom took out his pipe. Filling it with tobacco and lighting it he sat in the dark for several minutes, puffing gently and filling the air with a blue haze as he collected his thoughts.

"It is a strange turn of events," Tom mused. "Why would the sheriff be out here talking to one of the men? Why would he walk into camp rather than drive?" Tom made a note in his spiral notebook, replaced it in his coat. "Was he really trying to hide, or was that fellow feeling some paranoia from living the transient life himself for so long?"

After a few minutes Tom left the shack. Stepping outside he knocked the ashes from his pipe onto the soggy ground. Then, he himself walked into the transient camp.

The camp was set back just a short way from the river. To the east of the encampment and clustered at the base of a hill defining the river's flood plain was a small farm site. Neat and well maintained, it showed the pride of its Norwegian homestead occupants.

As Tom began walking he saw the transient camp itself was set up in a quadrangle and looked every bit like a small military base. On the left as he entered Tom saw a large warehouse and the foremen's quarters. At right angles to these was a row of six barracks to accommodate the three hundred-odd men living at this job site. In a row across the south end of the encampment stood the infirmary, the sanitation building which the men referred to as the shower shack, and the nearest building was the officers' quarters. By itself along the axis of the river stood the mess hall which could accommodate as many as two hundred-fifty men at a time.

The encampment was set about a quarter of a mile south of the roadway, where in only a few months a modern tarmac road would run across the valley. As Tom walked between the buildings he thought of the little man's observation that it seemed strange for the sheriff to walk in over the muddy ground rather than drive.

Tom passed through the camp and into the wooded area behind the sanitation building. Close behind the row of buildings was a deep wide ravine into which the wastewater from the sanitation building drained before running into the river. Tom followed the ravine's high bank toward the river.

As he stood in the near darkness listening to the gurgling river Tom realized his informant had been only partially right. Yes, there had been a light snow, but here in the trees the temperature hadn't changed nearly as much as in the more exposed areas. The snow which had fallen had somehow missed the large woods just below the shower shack. Cautiously, Tom walked back and forth through the trees. Then Tom spotted the cigarette butts; first one, then two, three, four altogether, lying in the snow.

As he looked closer he saw the broken matches scattered on the ground. Bent in the middle, they looked as if the smoker had struck the matches against the book cover without removing the match. Tom recognized this as a method frequently used by men in construction work. Hadn't he done the same himself more than once?

Mixed in with the now almost obliterated tracks of those men who had stood here speaking on an earlier date were the delicate footprints of the squirrels which had come seeking nuts or camp scraps that the men sometimes liked to feed them. And mixed with these were tracks showing a small cottontail rabbit had passed through, probably unnoticed, probably as recent as this morning.

In a bare spot on the ground, near a large box elder tree, Tom spotted a dark stain in the soggy earth. He brushed his fingers through the stain, then held them up to his eyes, recognizing that the dark stain was blood. Later it was proved that his curiosity was well founded. Tom removed a handkerchief from his pocked, wiped his fingers, before replacing the blood stained square in his pocket.

Tom turned to leave, expecting to find no more clues, but something at the river's edge caught his attention. He scrambled down the bank, cursing to himself as the muddy soil slopped into his shoes and oozed through his fingers as he sought to maintain his balance. Then, when he found his balance once more, he knelt beside the open river. From its ice crusted shore he withdrew a long steel blade nearly buried in the bank. Taking a glove from his pocket and slipping it on his hand Tom delicately held the cold steel as he scrambled back up the embankment. Looking neither left nor right he walked quickly out of the camp.

That night, Tom lay awake a long time. Now, he faced a true dilemma. He was beginning to believe, by this time, that the sheriff was involved with something but where could Tom turn? Certainly not to the sheriff, who Tom thought might be guilty of something—maybe something as serious as murder. He didn't think he could bring the evidence to a deputy, for certainly, the deputies—who were hired by Carl Brown—would owe their allegiance to him.

Tom felt as if he were trying to assemble a puzzle where all the pieces were the same size, shape, and color, and he didn't even have all of the pieces. *Ernie run over and left dead on the highway; Warren appearing to be guilty of hit and run, someone viciously beaten to death, the clues all pointing to Warren.* "But what clues?" Tom questioned. So far there was only the sheriff's word that Warren was guilty, combined with witnesses who had seen Warren and Timmy Coyle arguing earlier. But this didn't make a man guilty.

The sheriff and his deputies had beaten Warren viciously when they had arrested him for the murder of Timmy Coyle but all the while Warren swears that he is innocent. "When they arrested me I didn't even know why the sheriff and his deputies were there," he had said. "They dragged me from the truck, and before my feet hit the ground Carl kicked me in the balls. When I doubled over at the pain he kicked me again, and I felt a rib break when his knee slammed into my chest. I knew then I was in real trouble. I don't remember that either of the deputies did anything except hold me or pick me back up when I fell."

"The next thing I remember is seeing the sheriff pull his club from his belt, yelling something, I haven't any idea what. I lifted my arms to protect my head; that's when he must have broken my arm, with the club. I remember he hit me several times with the night stick. I couldn't understand what was happening. Every time I tried to ask the sheriff something he screamed and hit me again. Finally, I guess I just passed out. I just can't figure out why they wanted to beat me up."

And, Tom wondered, *Where is the justification for that beating which had put Warren in the hospital with broken ribs and a broken arm, not to mention all the damage to his face.*

Now we're faced with the disappearance of one of the transients; and a witness who is unwilling to come forward but stating that maybe the missing man and the sheriff had an argument or fight of some kind. Supporting this man's theory is the blood I found on the ground and the car bumper I pulled from the river. Do these mean anything? After all, the blood could have come from anywhere.

But, he responded to his own argument, *the camp cook said he found the blood there right after the possible argument. I just don't know what it all means.*

Finally Tom laid his notebook aside and slept. The hollow ticking of the shiny Electrolux clock on the nightstand which soothed him to sleep woke him with its steady beat at six o'clock the next morning. As he lay collecting his thoughts, he suddenly reached for the phone. To the desk clerk who answered Tom spoke. "I'd like you to connect me with this number in Washington, D.C......"

Chapter

Twenty-nine

In the hotel dining room Tom waited for a response to his early morning call. He had taken a table in a corner as far from the dining traffic as possible, and over the next several hours, he studied his notes of the past days, rewriting them several times, adding questions to his list as new possibilities came to his mind.

Working studiously over his notes, Tom smiled as, from time to time he caught sight of the haughty waitress who was trying hard to ignore him, but when he called occasionally for coffee, she craned her neck, trying to remain aloof and inconspicuous as she eavesdropped. Tom however, continued to keep his secrets, shifting papers, or leaning at just the right angle to obscure her vision.

Once or twice Tom went to the phone, talked for a moment, and returned to continue his study. Just as Tom was beginning to get impatient at his inability to solve a particular problem he sensed another presence. Looking up, he watched as an elderly man approached. Tall, with straight silver hair, the man carried himself like a king, gliding across the room. With his hat in hand he approached Tom, who automatically rose in deference to the stranger.

"Good morning young man. I'm John Chamberlin and I've been asked to meet with you."

"It's a pleasure to meet you, sir," Tom responded to the stranger's introduction. Tom sensed immediately that this man was here in response to his early morning call. "Thank you for seeing me. Please, have a seat; coffee?" Tom was immediately at ease; he sensed by the judge's demeanor that he had found an ally.

Tom's guest waited until the awestruck waitress, who couldn't believe she was seeing His Honor the Judge with this stranger, treating him almost as an equal, left them to their privacy. "Tom, you have a powerful friend or three back in Washington. I've had several calls today from men I thought had forgotten me."

"I'm sorry if I've caused you any inconvenience, sir. Of course, when I made my call I had no way of knowing my request would funnel right back here. The best I had hoped for was finding someone at the capital who might be available to bring me some help."

"I served a couple of terms in Washington before I became a judge, Tom. As it happens, your friends in Washington just recognized the coincidence of my living right here. It's something of a semi-retirement, being a Federal judge out here. But as a matter of fact, I'm pleased to be included in whatever is going on."

"I grew up in this valley, Tom. For me it was the center of the universe before I went off to the University of Minnesota." There was a glow of pride, pleasant memories on his face. "Well, as young men will do, I got my education and forgot to go home. I practiced law in Saint Paul for a while. Then, I ran successfully for the state legislature a few years later. It was an exciting time, lots happening in those days. A couple of terms there however, and I thought I was ready for the big time and moved to the Federal arena. Finally, though, I thought about retiring, coming back to my valley."

"As it happened however, instead of retiring, I was appointed to the Supreme Court. I guess, they were pretty hard up at the time!" He laughed. "When I had a heart attack a few years ago I decided if I was ever going to enjoy my valley again I'd better high-tail it back here."

"Once in a while though, something comes up, like the little problem you have, and, well, when I can help out I do what I can."

"Your honor," Tom began, "thank you for taking the time to see me and to listen to my theory. When I called my old boss this morning I had no Idea where it might lead, but I've stumbled into something very puzzling. I'll try the best I can to cut right to the meat of the problem. Then, if anything I say makes sense to you, I'll tell you what I think needs to be done."

"Fill me in as much as you see fit, Tom. I'll let you know as we go along what my thoughts are."

"I know at first this will all seem unusual, your honor, but as I begin to get all the pieces on the table I think you'll agree that some of the questions which have been bothering me need to be pursued and answered before Warren goes to trial."

"When I came to Montevideo a couple of weeks ago, my only thought was to retrieve the body of my brother Ernie. He was a teamster from the Lac Qui Parle Dam project and was killed in January. Ernie and I had been very close growing up. He was like a father to me. The day I came home from the Navy I found out he had died in a hit and run accident. All I could think of doing was to get him home and buried next to our father. I suppose I could have just had the body shipped home, but it just didn't seem right. I felt like I could repay Ernie in some way if I came and escorted him home in person, I guess that's a little silly, isn't it?"

"To the contrary, Tom. If more people still had such a strong sense of family, maybe our country wouldn't have been so badly hurt in the depression. We seem to have lost our compassion, the feeling of being responsible for our own actions. I admire your motive, Tom."

"Well, sir, I came here fully expecting to vent my anger on the man who had run over him. In my mind I saw someone vile, irresponsible. But almost from the beginning it felt like something was out of place. The first thing I heard when I got off the train was about Ernie's death, the then the murder of someone else in town."

"It's not unusual for someone like your stationmaster to spread the gossip with such a gleam in his eye. Gossips are the same all over the world, aren't they? At first I didn't think it unusual for the sheriff to show such animosity against the man in his cell, especially when he told me there was compelling evidence this same young man murdered someone else in cold blood only a week later."

The afternoon wore on as the two men traded queries and responses. Tom methodically placed the pieces of his puzzle before the judge. From time to time the retired jurist shook his head in disbelief, occasionally added a point Tom had not noted. He wondered not only at the unbelievable story unfolding, but at the tenacity of the young man across the table. "He's like a wolf stalking its prey, following an elusive rabbit's trail through brushy bottom lands; only I don't think it's a rabbit he's after. I don't know why he didn't just take his brother's body and leave, but I have a feeling we're all going to benefit from his decision to try figure and this all out."

"Tom, I have a feeling you have a plan of some kind. Where is this all going?" Although John Chamberlin was no longer a young man, his mind was clear and quick. His response to Tom's observations left no doubt in Tom's mind that as a legislator this man had been a mover and a shaker, someone who saw the real problems and demanded immediate solutions.

"As I became more curious about the circumstances of the two deaths I began asking questions. Of course, it didn't take long for Sheriff Brown to learn I had been doing some investigating on my own. He came down on me like smell on bad meat, I can tell you. He told me he had the evidence that Warren was guilty; that I had no business stirring things up; that I should take my brother's body and hightail it back to Ohio."

"I'm sure the sheriff was still smarting from last week when I brought Doc Wilson to the jail and demanded that Warren be hospitalized. You know, for a moment there in the jail I thought the sheriff might even get violent with me. I saw something in his eyes that afternoon that scared me. He sure didn't seem much like the man who had sent the compassionate telegram to my mother telling her how sorry he was about Ernie's death."

"As I became accepted a little more by the local people I began to hear stories about the sheriff," Tom continued. "Certainly by now you've heard them too, how the sheriff disliked farmers and how he disliked transients even more."

"I could have been knocked over with a feather, when I heard he hated the Indians enough to have shot one last year in a neighboring county. My God, Your Honor, he was a deputy sheriff there, and from everything I've heard, the shooting was more nearly murder than self-defense. Everyone in the whole area seems to know that he would frequently pick up the Indian women in the bars. And the Indians, at least, knew how he would physically and sexually assault them before taking them home. After he killed that man in Yellow Medicine County, he was fired, but the next thing you know he's the sheriff right here in Montevideo!"

"Tom, I guess sometimes it takes a stranger to make us look at ourselves. You may not believe this… as a matter of fact, when I listen to the facts you've laid out, I'm not sure I can believe it myself, but I was instrumental in getting Carl appointed sheriff."

"The sheriff in Chippewa County gets elected, just like most of the country, of course. As it happened, Dan Fraughton, who'd been sheriff, for maybe twenty years, died of a heart attack. For some reason Carl seemed like the kind of young new blood we needed to put some backbone into our law enforcement."

"This area out here is growing, and with all the activity going on around here these days, some of us felt Dan had been too soft. We've been seeing all kinds of drifters; sometimes hobos came right into town looking for handouts. Since the depression, we've been hit as hard as anyplace. There's no work in a town like Montevideo that isn't somehow, connected to farming or railroading, you know. When the big war got over, Tom, we started seeing some of the vets riding the rails, stopping off here hoping for Lord knows what kind of miracle, but we didn't have anything to offer them."

"When we started seeing our crime rate going up I suppose we just wanted to protect ourselves. When Dan retired we were looking for someone a little stronger. It seemed to us that Carl had a reputation of keeping riff-raff in check, and I guess we were willing to overlook all the rumors about him in order to gain a little safety. But the way you've put it to me, I can see we might have created our own danger."

Tom glanced at his notes again; then he leaned forward as he continued. "When I was at the dam site yesterday one of the men from the camp approached me. Now, this man doesn't want to be identified, but he told me of seeing Sheriff Brown at the transient camp talking with one of the workers. Afterward, the sheriff left. The other man, a fellow named Ollie Martin, disappeared."

"Later that day I followed this man's directions and went into the woods to the place the meeting was supposed to have taken place. I discovered cigarette butts and matches where they had talked, as well as blood on the ground. At the edge of the river I found a piece of bumper from a Model A Ford partially buried in the riverbank."

"I stayed awake a long time last night trying to fit everything together. When I woke up this morning the pieces started to fall into place."

"After I called Washington, I went to the coroner and asked to see the photos taken of Ernie after his death. I suppose he was in the right, refusing me access as he did, but I think some of the answers are in those photos and it was then I realized just what needs to be done in order to clear this up."

"Tom, you just tell me what I can do. I can guarantee I'll bring as much pressure to bear as I possibly can."

In the next few minutes Tom, referring frequently to his notebook, outlined his proposed course of action. When he finished he sat quietly while John Chamberlin gazed at him.

"Here's the way we'll handle this, Tom...."

CHAPTER
THIRTY
March 4, 1938

It had seemed such a simple task, to take the train to Minnesota, get Ernie's body and bring him home to bury beside Dad. But what strange events seem to be taking place in this little town. Tom smiled as the long nosed waitress served more coffee. *My, haven't we changed our attitude*, Tom thought as she left. After Tom's meeting with Judge Chamberlin he had no trouble with service anywhere in the hotel.

Tom continued to make notes in the small spiral book he kept. In Washington, he had gotten into the habit of outlining or graphing problems he had to solve. It didn't take long with the intelligence group for him to learn how frequently seemingly unrelated facts, when combined properly were in fact connected.

What started as a neat outline often ended a mishmash of crossing lines connecting cogent points which individually had made little sense. But the method had frequently proved itself when Tom solved mysterious problems such as the one he found here. This morning several answers filled the spaces which had previously been voids.

Tom had talked with Jeanne several times about the night of Ernie's death and about the night of Timmy Coyle's death. They had talked of the relationship between Warren and Jeanne, and he felt now he was beginning to know and understand them both. Tom found them easy to like. "This is not the way I thought it would be," he thought again, "but the longer I'm here the easier it is to believe Warren is innocent. But if Warren is innocent, why is the sheriff so determined to place the guilt on Warren?"

Yesterday, after meeting with the judge, Tom and Jeanne had driven in Warren's coupe to Wegdahl. He hadn't said as much, but he wanted to see if she could really retrace the route Warren and she were supposed to have taken. He also wanted to find out how long it took to make the trip, "just in case…" he had thought.

The two of them had left town following the east side of the railroad tracks, past the switching yards, then we followed the gravel road south. "See, here…this is the Peterson farm I told you about. We almost turned around here, but Warren was still so angry I didn't want him to go back."

As they went on, Jeanne pointed out the desert-like stretch where the uncultivated land was full of cactus and large rocks looming up through the snow now, but in the summer it looked like a desert with all the spiny plants clinging to the rocky ground.

They had come into Wegdahl. Tom turned the car up a narrow grade which wound up through the low hills east of town. "This is where we stopped. We…talked for a while here as we watched out over the valley." She blushed profusely, and while Tom looked immediately away to allow her time to recover from her embarrassment, he knew their talk had been of a physical nature.

Why am I jealous? Tom asked himself. *After all, they're keepers of their own lives. And I can certainly see how she could make a man thankful to be a man!* For a moment he remembered his own short romance in Washington, D.C.

"We...talked here for about a half hour, I guess." Jeanne continued, "Tom, I don't understand why Sheriff Brown is trying to do this to Warren. It's almost as if he has a grudge against him, wants to get even with him for something. I can't believe the way he beat Warren up when they arrested him the second time. They came right out to Swift's and dragged him out of his truck."

That was a puzzle, all right. Tom had gone out to the plant at Swift's only a couple of days ago to see if anyone there had seen the sheriff come for Warren; one of the questions in his notebook. Although no one came forward, Tom had a feeling there had been a witness. In this maze of buildings he felt sure someone must have seen or heard something, but so far he had had no luck in locating that person.

How could they have dragged Warren off the job in daylight, people working inside and out, without a single witness to the violent beating Warren had received? There were still too many unanswered questions here, Tom thought.

Why can't I find out what proof the sheriff holds against Warren? And what about Jeanne? Jeanne sounds so convincing about where she and Warren were the night of Coyle's death, and she just doesn't seem like the kind of a girl who can lie well.

"Jeanne, everyone I talk to tells me what a bigot Sheriff Brown is. He rants and raves about transients, the farmers, and the Indians, all the while taking advantage of the Indian women. And it seems like the sheriff takes advantage of everyone he deals with. Can you shed any light for me?"

Jeanne, although unaware the sheriff surely didn't like Warren, indicated she was unaware of Carl's attitudes. "I just know every time I'm alone when I see him he's more than nice to me, but something in his eyes frightens me, and whenever I'm with Warren the sheriff just glowers at us."

After a few minutes Tom turned the car down the hill again, passing through Wegdahl, across the bridge, then a little further turning north towards Montevideo. As the afternoon wore on Tom traced the icy route, carefully negotiating the slippery curves Jeanne and Warren professed to have taken the night of Timmy's death. Tom was beginning to believe that in spite of the sheriff's position, Warren just might be innocent, as he claimed.

On the surface everything seems absolutely cut and dried, he thought. *Ernie was in the bar having a few drinks, and why not? Jeanne and Warren, by their own admission, were there partying and drinking with their friends; very normal, except for the storm raging around them. Then, they left in the midst of the blizzard. When the sheriff left only minutes later he found Ernie's body already covered with snow, the clear imprint of Warren's tires running across Ernie's body. The side of Ernie's head was caved in, and he had been dead for only a short while."* Although the description was certainly factual, something didn't seem quite right to Tom. *"The following morning Sheriff Brown had arrested Warren, and in his enthusiasm to enforce the law, had conscripted the county snowplow to help get him to the Amundson farm. But why was the sheriff so incensed about arresting Warren that he couldn't wait for the storm to end? Surely there were others who needed attention, more immediately than Warre, who was released from jail the following Wednesday.*

According to reports, on Saturday night, only days before I arrived, Timmy Coyle confronted Warren downtown by the new Monte Theatre. When Warren was dragged away from Timm, in the midst of Timmy's violent threats, there had been several witnesses. The next morning they found Timmy Coyle's body in the alley, with his head split open and several bones broken. The sheriff immediately sought Warren, locating him on Monday.

But when the sheriff and his deputies arrested Warren, why had they beaten him so unmercifully and totally out of proportion with any resistance Tom could imagine the young man might have shown. Although there seemed to be enough evidence to at least point a finger toward Warren, it seemed to Tom to be only circumstantial at best. Other than the sheriff, and Timmy Coyle's cadre of dimwits, not a person confirmed Warren's propensity toward violence as voiced by the sheriff. To all who knew him, Warren was quiet, self-confident, easy going.

The way his eyes pleaded to me and the sincerity in his voice when he told me he wasn't guilty...it's as if the sheriff hates Warren so much he would do anything to get rid of him. But why would that be? Tom thought. *Why would a man with a position as secure as Sheriff Brown be so vehement about Warren's guilt and still not be able to show any concrete evidence?*

At ten-thirty Tom was summoned to the phone. For several minutes he listened, as John Chamberlin explained the actions he had taken, how Tom now should follow up. "He'll be expecting you within the hour, Tom. If your suspicions are correct, call me; I'll be here most of the day." Tom hurriedly scratched a note in his book

and in less than a minute was on his way to pay another
visit to the coroner.

CHAPTER
THIRTY-ONE
March 4, 1938

When he first saw the photographs spread on the desk Tom wasn't sure he could go through with his plan. The photos in the coroner's file showed that Ernie had indeed been run over by an automobile. Not only were they far more graphic than he expected, but they were also of his brother. It was like volunteering to have a nightmare. The photos showed the imprint of the tires from Warren's car, and they seemed conclusive as far as Tom was concerned.

It wasn't just the bloody wound across the side of Ernie's head; the coroner's photographs also pointed out tire bruises across Ernie's back and both arms, broken, bruises staring up at Tom who now had to accept that Warren was guilty of running over Ernie just as the sheriff said. In spite of his pleas, in spite of Jeanne's admonitions that Warren couldn't leave Ernie lying in the snow, the photographs did not lie. In a way Tom was sad; he had actually wanted Warren to be innocent.

"Now, let me see the other photographs."

"Mister Hall, I'm not sure you want to do this. I've got to tell you; young Coyle's body looks a lot worse than your brother's."

That may be, but I have to see for myself." Tom hoped he was really ready for this; maybe he should just leave well enough alone, get out of this place.

No, I've come this far, and I'm going to see it through. To the coroner, "Something keeps nagging me, doesn't quite add up, and I need to know the real truth before I leave. Of course, I want my brother's killer to come to justice, but in my gut something tells me we're not seeing all the facts."

The coroner unwillingly spread the second collections of gory photographs on the table before Tom. "I get to see lots of bodies on this job, but I don't think I'll ever get used to looking at them. Especially when they come to me looking like this poor young man did."

"Oh, Jesus," Tom murmured as he looked at the photos of Timmy Coyle. He felt weak, light in the stomach as he groped for a chair and sat. For a minute he couldn't look at the photos spread before him. Then he steeled himself to his task and rose again to look at the vivid record spread before him. "Could you tell which blow actually killed him?"

"Not really. Several of the blows, here…here…or this one, could easily have done it. It looks like the killer just set about to torture him as much as he could before he finally put him down for keeps."

Tom had to concentrate in order to keep his head clear, to think of the photos as something other than a young man his own age, in order to complete the task. Then, as if jolted by a huge electrical shock he saw the beginning of the truth. "Dear, God, I don't believe it," he whispered as he settled once more into the chair. Tom's stomach felt hollow as he turned to the coroner. At first the solution had seemed very simple.

"I'd like you to look closely at these photos." He pointed to two. "Tell me if I'm seeing something that's not there. Or do you see what I think I see?"

As he rose to stand beside the coroner Tom heard the man's incredulous reply. "I'm not sure I can believe what I see, or that I understand even, how it could be possible."

Tom slid all the photos aside except two. There, side by side, the two photographs showed deep, wide excavations. Both wounds travelled at an angle across the right temple, crushing bone as some weapon passed, driving deep into the brain, and dragging sharp bone fragments along with the weapon as it pressed deeper, snuffing out life. Both wounds appeared to have been made by blows from a heavy steel bar, undoubtedly swung with tremendous force.

On the table before Tom and the coroner were the close-up photos showing the wounds. On the left was that of Timmy Coyle; on the right was the photo of Ernie Hall. The photos showed two dead men with nearly-identical head wounds.

CHAPTER
THIRTY-TWO

March 4, 1938

"When I looked at the photographs and realized the mark on Ernie's head was the same size and shape as the wounds suffered by Timmy Coyle at first I couldn't believe what I was looking at. Then I realized what had been bothering me all along." Tom and John Chamberlin faced each other in the latter's comfortable study. Seated in a large leather wing back chair matched by the one holding his host, Tom continued speaking above the pleasant crackling of the fireplace. "It took some time, however, to make the pieces fit, and of course a lot of this is still open to question, sure wouldn't stand up in any court at this point."

"The tire marks on Ernie's body, crossing his chest and arms certainly would have been enough to kill him; just the blow to his head by itself could have done it. Since it was assumed, from the beginning, that Warren was responsible for Ernie's death, apparently no one thought to compare the relationship between the two wounds. I was guilty as anyone else, just accepting what I was told by the sheriff, without investigating it for myself. But why would anybody think to question such a seemingly obvious solution?"

"Your Honor, unless I'm completely wrong in my observations, I think we'll find Warren Marshall innocent of both of the deaths he's charged with."

"Tom, how do you expect to convince the prosecutor, and for that matter Carl, of that?"

"I don't have the answer to that yet, Sir. But it's just too much coincidence to believe Ernie and Timmy Coyle were both killed by Warren, based on what those photos show. As I see it, here are the facts, which need be taken into consideration:

"Number one, Timmy was beaten to death with a section of a car bumper. We have the murder weapon, or the police do, but there are no fingerprints, no way to connect anyone to the weapon."

"Fact number two, Ernie was run over by Warren car. His tire tracks were definitely on Ernie's body, as well as packed into the snow nearby. I'm convinced however, that the blow to Ernie's head was what killed him. There are a couple of additional considerations here also."

"That blow to his head looks surely to have been made the same way as the one to the side of Timmy Coyle's head; both were struck on the right side of the head, and the photos show both blows struck from almost identical angles." The judge withdrew his gaze from Tom and looked at the two glossy pictures on the coffee table before him.

"Yes, so far this makes sense, Tom," he responded.

"Add to this the location of the tire tracks Warren's car left on Ernie's body. If...I say if, Warren's car knocked Ernie to the ground, actually to the snow covered roadway, I think it would be impossible for his car to have crossed over Ernie's chest and arms as the photographs show it to have done. There aren't any bruises lower on his body where a fender or bumper might have struck him. And I can't imagine which part of his little Dodge might have opened Ernie's head as the photo shows."

"But where do you suppose this leaves us, Tom?"

"I'm still not sure, Your Honor, but I'm not finished yet. If we suppose for a moment that the section of car bumper found by Timmy's body was the actual murder weapon in both instances, and that Warren actually did kill Timmy Coyle, then we must believe that Ernie's death was a murder also, not just an accidental hit and run. Then we have a circumstance I find unbelievable."

"That would mean one of the following: that Warren, before he ran over Ernie and for some reason, unknown to us, jumped out of the car and struck Ernie a death blow...all before my brother could jump out of the way or defend himself. Then, to make the death look like an accident, Warren ran over the body, expecting the body to be discovered the next day or later if the storm continued. By that time it would be presumed that Ernie died from a hit and run.

On the other hand, we have to think Warren ran over Ernie accidently, then finding him still alive he panicked and struck him dead, leaving him on the roadway."

"I agree that your scenarios seem possible Tom, but it certainly doesn't seem very logical, does it?"

"I'm going to complicate this a little more, your Honor." Tom laid more photos on the table; then he reached for a towel-wrapped bundle at his feet. "You recall I told you about my trip out to Lac Qui Parle. I'd like you to see what I brought back," Gently Tom unrolled the towel, and used it to lay his find from the riverbank on the table. "You'll want to be careful not to touch it sir if you don't mind me cautioning you. I don't know if there are any fingerprints on this, but we'll treat it as though there may be some." When he laid the piece of Ford bumper next to the most recent photos Tom continued. "This is the item I pulled from the riverbank on Thursday; you'll notice it looks just like the one in the coroner's photo. That one," he tapped the picture with his finger, "is the weapon that murdered Timmy Coyle."

"When I pulled this one out of the snow I thought at first it might be the one used to kill Timmy, but then I remembered, the one used to kill Timmy had already been found in the snow, there in the alley. So what is the significance of this piece of steel bumper?"

"For a while, Tom, I was following right along with you, but I have to admit that right now I don't know where you're trying to lead me. I guess I'll just have to sit back and let you carry me along as you finish laying out your theory."

"Thank you, sir. I think in a few minutes you'll understand the significance of this. At least you will unless you think I'm absolutely crazy."

"Before I can prove or disprove anything, I need to have this bumper checked for fingerprints. That may solve our mystery. Or it may just leave us where we are. I also found some cigarette butts and match stubs when I was snooping around. I haven't the faintest idea whose they are, but maybe they'll mean something as we go along.

"I don't think the sheriff is going to able to help us, or perhaps I should say I don't think the sheriff will be willing to help us. But I wonder if, with your urging, we might get one of the deputies to help. I'm a little apprehensive, however. Since the sheriff hired both of the deputies I have to assume they will feel they owe their allegiance to him rather than to us."

"I think you can rest assured that Kenny will cooperate with us, Tom. You see, this is a small town; Kenny is married to my niece. If for no other reason, I believe he'll give us a hand any way he can. But before I bring him into this, just what do you think you're going to find?"

"I can't say for sure, but I think right now that instead of just one murder suspect, your Honor, we have three. The bumper here could possibly tell us for sure."

CHAPTER

THIRTY-THREE
March 5, 1938

"I feel a little like a traitor, Uncle John." The Right Honorable John Chamberlin, his niece's husband Kenny, and Tom Hall faced each other. Tom had just finished explaining his theory for Kenny's benefit, then had gone on to tell the deputy what role he needed to play before the day ended.

"Kenny, Tom here comes to us with credentials which are higher than any one you're likely to encounter ever again. I'm not going to go into detail, because what he's been involved in is too confidential to share even under these circumstances. But be assured he is qualified to make a valid judgment here. I concur in everything he has told you."

Tom felt slightly embarrassed at the accolades and interrupted to finish his request to Kenny. "As you no doubt know, Warren's trial is supposed to begin tomorrow. Of course, we can introduce any evidence we deem suitable during the trial, but if, I repeat, if we can clear this up, present enough facts before the trial to prevent it even beginning, I think everyone will be better off."

"We've come to you Kenny, because I believe somehow Sheriff Brown is mixed up in this." Although Kenny had seen and heard Tom's evidence and conjectures, he had not yet gotten this piece of information. "Kenny, the sheriff is not to know we have any questions whatsoever. I need to know if you know of any information, any notes the sheriff has made or any clues or other bits of information the sheriff did not give you. You work with the sheriff nearly every day. Can you think of anything he has done or said, recently that's unusual; unusual for him, that is?"

The split elm logs crackled in the fireplace, sending flickering light across Kenny's face as he spoke. It was easy to see he was uneasy at being put on the spot and asked to inform about his boss's activities. "Carl has always been pretty secretive, of course. I suppose that's from having to deal with so many of people's problems that need to stay private. But lately he sure has been hard to work with. He just seems to be mad all the time, ready to bite my head off for the slightest reasons."

"The only time he's been in a really good mood seems to be on Monday mornings." He hesitated. "I guess by now you know he spends Sunday nights, ah…, relaxing."

"We don't have to be delicate here this morning, Kenny. Tom and I know that on Sundays the sheriff is usually in some small town or other, drinking or whoring."

"Yes Sir. Well, other than bragging about that, he's been pretty ornery lately."

"I think he might know something, or be hiding some evidence from us, Kenny. Have you noticed anything to lead you to think that might be true?"

"Well…you know, now that you mention it, he's really gotten upset a couple of times when I was looking for something on his desk. He's yelled, of course that's not unusual, but now that I'm thinking about it, he keeps his desk locked now and he never did before."

John Chamberlin and Tom exchanged glances. Then the judge turned to Kenny. "Kenny, can you get into that desk? Better yet, I'd like Tom to have a look. Of course we need to be sure Carl won't walk in on you while you're doing it. Do you think you can arrange that?"

The young deputy seemed to pale. The last thing he could imagine wanting was to have the sheriff walk in while he and Tom Hall were rifling his desk. The sheriff's wrath surely wouldn't stop with firing him. "I...I don't know, Sir. I mean I really want to help, but..."

"Your Honor, Kenny...I think I have the answer. First of all, we're running out of time, so I think we need to do this as soon as possible. But, other than spending a couple of hours at the jail on Sundays, we do know that the sheriff is almost always heading out of town by sunset on Sundays. I think that once he's left we would have pretty easy access to whatever we need."

"I have a couple of errands to do," Tom continued while looking at the young deputy, "but after that I'm going to be at the hotel. Kenny, if you'll call me after you're sure the sheriff has gone for the day I'll come to the jail. I'll meet you there, and together we can have a look in that desk." Turning to the judge Tom continued, "There is one thing in particular you can do Sir, just to protect our position in case it becomes necessary. I'd like a search warrant, for both the sheriff's office and his hotel room."

CHAPTER
THIRTY-FOUR

Sunday night had always been Carl's night to howl and prowl. He knew when you know all the night spots, there's always entertainment to be found,. It was an old habit, Sunday night, begun when his duties as deputy sheriff in Granite Falls kept him busy on Friday and Saturday, when the civilians were on the prowl. Carl was in a good mood and ready to celebrate.

Carl was convinced he had finally planted all the seeds he could in the proof of Warren's guilt. It had taken some doing, but he had prevailed. That goddamn Tom Hall had given him some trouble; he finally had to threaten him before the guy agreed to butt his nose out of the investigation.

"It looks good, indeed," Carl thought as he crossed his room. "Although I didn't find just the evidence I wanted, I've sown all the seeds of doubt that I can. Tomorrow the trial starts and it looks to me like Warren's going in the can." Standing in front of the mirror and brushing his hair one last time, then stretching the wrinkles out of his shirt, Carl was now ready for a night on an Indian. Vulgar as it might have sounded to anyone else, it was Carl's definition of a good time; he had been thinking of this for hours.

Dum da dum dum," he hummed. "What a night this will be." Carl was experiencing the best mood he had been in for several days. "Dum da dum dum dum. Yes sir, I think tonight it will be Hazel Run. I haven't been there in some time. We haven't had any snow for a while now, the roads should be clear. I remember that little squaw from down by Morton that gets over to Hazel Ron a lot. Maybe she'll show up tonight. Yep, it'll be Hazel Run.

Yes, it had been a very good week, all right. Carl felt that he had cut off all of Tom Hall's questions; answered them good and clean, that was sure. *I'm just going down to Hazel Run, find me that little gal from Morton and have me a little poontang for Carl tonight.* He was smiling broadly as he headed for the door, picked up the bottle from the table and whisked down the last two swallows from the glass beside it.

I think I'll head out highway two-twelve, then drop down to Boyd to see what's happening down there, have a couple of drinks then swing into Clarkfield. "It's gonna be a great night, Carl thought. *A great night.*

"Then from Clarkfield I can head across to Hazel Run; just a nice easy drive," he said aloud. Carl knew all the local back roads. *If I don't get lucky in Hazel Run I can always head back over to Granite Falls. That little redhead that works for the Car dealer in Granite Falls is always happy to see me if worse comes to worst.* But it was the Indian girl Carl had on his mind. *At least the night won't be a complete waste.* Then off through the night Carl sped.

It looked like a very good night for Carl. He knew things were going his way, and had no doubt that Warren was going to go to prison. After he was gone there'd be plenty of time to get serious about Jeanne. He knew it wouldn't take long to win her over. The women just couldn't resist him Carl knew; Jeanne would be no different than the others once she had the right incentives.

Tonight Carl felt free as a bird, king of the mountain, and was off to his old stomping grounds.

As soon as he received Kenny's call Tom went directly to the jail. He could understand the young man's nervousness, and just smiled as Kenny stammered and tried to make small talk. A quick look through the oak file cabinet convinced Tom there was nothing to of importance there, and he moved to the sheriff's desk. It was locked.

"I imagine it's too much to hope that you have a key for this?" He was already in motion when the deputy confirmed this. In just a few seconds Tom opened the desk with a small tool taken from his jacket. Then, methodically, he began searching. Several layers down in the large bottom drawer, Tom found the packet containing the evidence he had hoped to find. He was still faced with unanswered questions, but here, in his hand, in the cellophane bag, he believed he had enough compromising evidence to keep Warren from going to prison. In the bag were three matches, bent while still in the matchbook while the smoker had lit his cigarette, then ripped out and dropped to the ground. The matches from the alley where Timmy Coyle died were the same as those Tom found in the snow at the construction site.

CHAPTER
THIRTY-FIVE

Carl had his couple of drinks in Clarkfield; good stiff drinks that warmed him through. It was moonshine he'd gotten just this week. *And it really set a man all aglow,* he thought. Clarkfield was kind of quiet though, since a lot of the boys liked to stay home on Sunday night to recover from Saturday's drinking, to get their heads and their bellies back in shape for work on Monday. So Carl jumped back into his Ford and headed down the highway to his next stop.

By the time he got to Hazel Run that night Carl was feeling no pain. There was a ruddy glow on his cheeks and red cast to his eyes; Carl was getting deep in his cups, as the saying goes. It was quiet when he arrived at the bar in Hazel Run. Carl shot a game of pool with one of the boys from Granite Falls who'd been out just driving around the countryside. Then he slid onto a stool at the bar and spent a half hour playing six, five four with the bartender and one of the other Sunday night regulars.

About nine-thirty the door opened, and as the cool draft reached across to Carl he turned to see Mary Dove, the young girl from Hazel Run, enter with a group of her friends, some white, and some Indian.

Carl never could understand how those white kids could hang out with those *damn Indians.* For some reason it never occurred to Carl that these people had interests similar to his own. The only thing that did occur to Carl when it came to Indians was that he liked to throw the women in the back seat of his Ford and screw his brains out. If they argued, he knew how to bring them around to his way of thinking. "Fill them with liquor," he thought, then take them home. But not before you stop in the grove; not before you find a place to loosen your load." And, tonight looked like a good night for Carl to loosen his load.

Carl ordered two more Cokes from the bar, grabbed them from the bartender and with his plain, brown-wrapped bottle of moonshine he crossed the room to join Mary Dove at her crowded table.

Before long most of the others at the table had moved, deserting Mary Dove to Carl. It was one thing to go out on a Sunday night and have a good time, but whenever Carl showed up the mood changed. Carl's mind was dirty, and Carl's mouth was vulgar. They knew that before very long in some way he would run them off. So, feeling only slightly guilty at deserting their companion, one by one they moved to other tables, leaving Mary Dove alone with Carl.

The big Wurlitzer at the back of the bar continued to blast their ears with its scratchy music and Carl continued to pour his moonshine liberally into the Coke bottles in front of him. By now, Carl was enraptured by Mary Dove. As he stared into her deep brown eyes images of their later encounter flashed through his mind. Reflected there he saw images of Jeanne beneath him, welcoming him drawing him into her.

Carl didn't notice later when the door opened and John Walking Bear entered the room with the two young men who called him Uncle. They sat quietly at a corner table, sipping at their drinks as the night wore on.

Tonight however, all three men were drinking their Coca Cola without the benefit of the moonshine. They seemed not to notice that once more Carl Brown was mauling and pawing one of their young Indian women. They kept their eyes averted from Carl's booth, but occasionally one or the other would flick his eyes quickly toward Carl, and occasionally they would flinch as some vulgarity which Carl whispered or yelled across the room for all to hear.

As the night wore on the crowd that arrived with Mary Dove left, seeking lighter entertainment. As they bid Mary Dove goodnight, her friends seemed to sense that any attempt to pry her from Carl would be in vain and feeling bad that once again Carl would be able to inflict his will on their friend, even beating her up as he had done on occasion. The boisterous mood they held earlier in the evening had been destroyed and they abandoned her as they left the bar.

Now, only Carl and Mary Dove in their booth, and John Walking Bear, were alone in the room with the bartender. John Walking Bear's two young companions were waiting outside for their uncle. They had sensed that soon Carl would be leaving, and not wanting to be obvious in their departure, had arranged to leave one at a time, to meet again later at John Walking Bear's car.

John Walking Bear rose from his table and walked to the bar. After a few moments conversation with the bartender he turned toward the door, ignoring the last remaining couple. With a pleasant smile and a wave of his hand he bid the bartender goodnight as he left the tavern.

A few minutes later the bartender came by Carl's booth. As it was now nearing midnight, he suggested that Carl and Mary Dove would like to take a Coke or two with them so that he, who had been working all night while the others had been enjoying themselves, could go to bed.

Carl pushed himself into a more upright position in the booth, and slurring his words as he spoke, agreed that perhaps it was, indeed, time for them to head out. At this a frightened look flashed across Mary Dove's face, as if for the first time she recognized that she was alone with Carl. She realized now that her weakness earlier had left her in his grasp and that her friends had gone home. She also felt a certain conviction as she looked at Carl that the least she could expect, if she were very lucky, was for Carl to violently make love to her. "What a laugh that is," she realized too late as she looked at him. "Carl doesn't know the meaning of the word love."

Somehow she was unable to fight off Carl's advances. He had an overpowering personality, and the strength of it drained away her resolve whenever he showed up. Several times he had found her in Hazel Run or Canby or Granite falls, and from the very first time it had always been the same. Instead of taking her directly home he found a quiet logging road into the woods along the Minnesota River close to her home. There, in the somber darkness of the woods Carl pressed her into submission. It seemed more nearly rape than making love; she couldn't recall that she had ever really consented to Carl's advances. And it was fortunate too, that it was near her home because on more than one occasion, Carl had pushed her from the car when he was finished with his pleasure, laughing drunkenly, and telling her the walk home would be good for her.

"Perhaps tonight would be different," she thought, with little hope that it would be. "And perhaps tonight…perhaps it might even be good for me."

Carl took two fresh bottles of Coke and grabbing Mary Dove by the arm as much to steady himself as to guide her out the door, he left. No gentleman, Carl; Mary had to open her own door. Once inside the car, as he waited a few moments for the engine to warm, Carl pawed her viciously, his rough beard scraping abrasively against her neck. Then, with a loud laugh, he dropped the shift lever into first gear and sped out of the parking lot.

Tonight was indeed going to be a good night, thought Carl. He could hardly wait to get this damn squaw in the back seat of his Ford. From time to time he unscrewed the cap of the hot moonshine, drinking now directly from the bottle as he guided the car erratically down the highway. He then would pass it to Mary Dove, who would press the bottle to her mouth. But none of the liquor passed through her tightly clenched lips; she knew by now that Carl was very drunk and her own safety could be at stake.

Mile after mile they crossed Yellow Medicine County. Finally, Carl pulled off the highway onto a woodlot driveway. With his arm wrapped tightly around Mary Dove he gunned the Ford deeper into the woods, following a barely perceptible path. Finally after moving several hundred yards into the trees he switched off the engine and put out the lights.

Now, Carl thought, *this is what makes the night worthwhile, the best part of the whole week. This little Mary Dove, for an Indian she sure is a looker.* A momentary thought, *it's too bad she's not white. And she sure does like to please me.* Carl's ego blinded him to her fear and acquiescence, which he took to be willing submission to his virility. Groping and squeezing, Carl backed Mary Dove into the corner of the seat.

He fumbled with the buttons of her dress, dropping his head to her breasts, and scraping his course beard against her delicate skin. Mary Cove stifled a whimper which Carl mistook as a passionate response as he viciously squeezed her nipple. "O, my God, why can't he be just a little bit gentle?" Her only thought now was to try to get through this ordeal as rapidly as she could and hope for some small feeling of satisfaction. There was no backing away from Carl, there was no discussion of how she felt. There was only the animal, she realized now, venting his lust upon her. Soon he would rise up and enter her, slamming his body violently against hers with no regard whatsoever for her feelings, treating her as nothing more than an object to receive his seed.

Violent lust now moved Carl ahead at a rapid pace, seeking only his own satisfaction as he pawed at her. All the while he groped Mary Dove's body, tearing at her dress, bruising her delicate skin, visions of Jeanne flashed through his mind. In his mind now he saw Jeanne's delicate white breasts exposed to him. As he violently hurled Mary Dove to the seat, his drunken lust-filled brain raced on. "No need to climb in the back seat for this," Carl thought. As his hands fondled and kneaded Mary Dove's soft brown skin his liquor-soaked brain told him Jeanne's pale white skin was before him, her legs ready to thrust willingly upward as he entered her.

Carl's male organ throbbed in his pants and he knew that soon he had to enter Mary Dove or his own lust would cause him to cum in his pants. "That," his mind raced, "would be a real waste." He threw Mary Dove rudely against the seat, banging her shoulder against the steering wheel in his haste, his hot hands lifted her body onto the seat and he began fumbling with his belt.

CHAPTER
THIRTY-SIX
March 9, 1938

"Yes," Tom thought as he sat in the depot, "how differently things might have been." In the distance he could hear the great train signaling its arrival. It wasn't Tom's ego which felt good at the moment, but something much deeper that was satisfied. That he had been part of proving Warren's innocence, and that when he returned home now he could tell his mother the kind of man it really was who killed her son, Ernie.

And he could tell her many more things now, tell her things which might have remained unknown if he had only claimed Ernie's body and gotten back on the train, hurrying to bury him next to his father in Ohio.

He looked up slowly as the doors behind him swung open. Turning his head, he smiled as Jeanne and Warren walked toward him. Warren's face still showed a patchwork of green and purple around his swollen eyes as he smiled weakly. He was leaning on Jeanne's shoulder, moving stiffly as he stretched his hand out in thanks. "Jeanne convinced the doctor to let me out of the hospital in spite of the broken ribs. I had to see you again before you left. Tom, thank you so much. If not for you I'm certain that by now I'd be on my way to prison for something I didn't do. I just had to tell you goodbye and thank you again."

"We don't know how to thank you more than that, Tom," Jeanne said with a smile. In spite of the time she and Tom had spent together she was still shy toward him. "We'll always be in your debt for the investigating you did when no one else thought Warren might be innocent."

"Well, I can hardly say think nothing of it under the circumstances." He smiled at them. "You know, when I got off the train I was sure I would find someone in that jail I could immediately hate, that it would be easy to convince myself just by looking at him that he deserved to go to prison for killing my brother. That wasn't the case however, even though there was a moment later in the coroner's office when I was almost convinced of Warren's guilt. The first thing I knew, I found myself liking both of you. Then I found myself wondering just what the sheriff was up to. I guess if he hadn't been so busy trying to convince me Warren was guilty when I couldn't see any evidence to back it up I might just have gotten on the train the next day. I suppose you might say in this case the sheriff dug his own grave."

"I think you also need to thank Judge Chamberlin, who was willing to listen to my story before you came to trial, Warren," Tom was saying. "Perhaps he wouldn't have been so willing to act and see that the trial was called off with all charges against Warren dropped of course, if Sheriff Brown had shown up the morning of the trial, but by then I believe the facts surrounding the recent deaths had been brought to light."

It would be sufficient for Warren and Jeanne to know that Warren had been cleared of the charges against him. Tom had not fully explained the circumstances leading to Warren's release, nor did he intend to give out all the details of his own involvement. It had been necessary, however, to tell Warren and Jeanne most of the details regarding the sheriff's *accident*.

Jeanne wanted to see Carl, and all the grief he caused, laid to rest for the final time, and had insisted on attending Carl's funeral with Tom. News of Carl's death was released to the public early Monday morning as a tragic winter accident, and it was agreed that only those immediately involved would know the truth of his death.

"I think it's an acceptable idea also that the judge decided not to look for whoever it was who performed surgery of Sheriff Brown. We all have our suspicions about who is responsible, and I'm sure it wouldn't be too difficult to solve that particular question but everyone who knows the truth about the sheriff's death agrees that justice has finally been served, since its uncertain if Carl died from loss of blood or from the crash itself."

The path to Carl's justice had been sure and direct, and in this case the arrival was unexpected and final.

As the belt holding Carl's trousers loosened and the zipper started its journey downward, Carl was so consumed by the need to complete his task that only when the dome light came on did he realize the car door had swung open. "Wha..." he growled as he lurched upright.

Drunkenly disoriented, he looked over his shoulder, thinking he or Mary Dove had bumped the door handle and caused the door to pop open, but as he turned two strong dark hands reached into the car and violently grabbed him by the shirt. Carl's head slammed heavily against the steel door frame as he was dragged from his car. When he was thrown to the snowy ground, with his pants still around his legs Carl's unfocused eyes were wide, his confusion turned to anger as he looked up and saw the three tall swarthy men above him.

As Carl tried to lurch to his feet one of the men kicked him hard against his jaw, dropping him back onto the snowy ground. Then one of the younger men kneeled on Carl's biceps while the other scurried around to kneel over his feet, pinning him firmly to the ground between them.

John Walking Bear turned for only an instant to the car; "dress yourself, Mary Dove; leave. Don't look back...leave NOW I said."

Mary Dove, tears rushing down her cheeks, pulled her clothes close about her, fumbled for buttons; anything to cover her shame. Then, with her clothes pulled around her she turned and ran down the wooded track toward the highway, never looking back.

As Carl regained some of his composure and his mind began to clear he fought to bring the jumble of confused images into focus. Then his mind filled with anger. *What the hell is going on?* His mind rushed, not yet fully understanding what was happening. *Who do these goddamned Indians think they are? How did they find out I was here? What the hell are they going to do to me?*

When John walking Bear and his two young companions had left the bar in Hazel Run, they drove only a quarter mile down the road before pulling to the side of the road and turning off the headlights. Patiently they waited until Carl Brown's Ford sped by them in the night. There was no need for them to rush after him, for they knew where he was going. They had only to follow at a distance, keeping the headlights of Carl's Ford in sight.

Twenty minutes later they saw the headlights turn into the woods, and a moment later blink into darkness. They also turned off their headlights as their car slowed to a stop on the shoulder of the road, and cautiously they walked into the woods.

There was little chance anyone would see their car, left along the road, for it was now late at night. A half mile back they had passed a sign beside the road announcing their entrance into the Sioux Agency. Should anyone who would be likely to drive this road see John Walking Bear's car, they would think only that it had broken down and he had walked away for help.

The three men were also little concerned with the developments in the front seat of Carl's car. Although they tacitly disapproved of any white men bedding their women, Mary Dove was here of her own free will.

Their plan had been made earlier in the evening. Counting on Carl's lust and the amazing amount of alcohol the man had consumed to dull his senses, they had quietly approached the car. At the previously agreed signal one of the young men had pulled the door open and John Walking Bear wrenched Carl away from the young woman.

In the still night only the murmur of the Minnesota River nearby broke the silence as the three men stared at Carl.

The erection which had been Carl's considerable pride and had seemed to control all his actions only moments before had rapidly shrunk and now as he lay on the wet snowy ground with his pants around his knees, the tiny limp penis pointing up to the stars was the last thing on his mind. "Let me up, Damn it! Don't you know who I am?"

"Oh, yes. We know who you are, Sheriff Brown. For a long time we have known who you are. You are the defiler of our women. You are the man responsible for the many bruised faces of our women. You are the man who shot my brother, the father of William, who now holds your legs so firmly to the ground. Yes, Carl Brown," John Walking Bear continued, "we know very well who you are. But you see, we are no longer afraid of you, we know you are just a man as we are, and that you have bullied our people one time too many."

"We know that no one saw us follow you here, and that no one else knows where you have gone. We know that when the sun comes up tomorrow you will no longer be the mighty Sheriff Carl Brown."

Carl's eyes widened. He stammered "You can't do this. What are you going to do?" He tried to twist loose but was held firmly in place. "Let me go and I promise I'll never come back again. We can just forget this night ever happened." Straining upward against the tight grip of his two captors he screamed, "I'm sorry for what I did! I'm sorry I bothered your woman. I'm sorry I shot your brother. Don't hurt me," he whimpered as he lay writhing on the ground.

John Walking Bear was almost sad, but his deep brown eyes showed no forgiveness as he slowly leaned forward and looked directly into Carl's face. "There is a time you see, Sheriff, when people will not back up anymore. There is always a time when justice must be delivered."

"You have humiliated many of our people. First, when you lived in Granite Falls, when you swaggered around with your night stick which you used to club our young men. You thought they had too much to drink and had no pride. Then, you defiled our women, some willingly I agree. But the way you treated our women they could not look at their own image in the mirror. And how many homes have you destroyed, Carl Brown? You, who believe yourself to be so superior to all those around you....no, I think tonight justice will finally be served."

Then, as Carl watched, John Walking Bear reached behind him, under his coat, and quietly slid his knife from its sheath. "Oh no! Please don't kill me," he whimpered. "Certainly, you wouldn't kill me. Can't we talk this over?"

"No." John Walking Bear smiled. That would be too easy. And if we were to kill a sheriff all the law would come looking for us, wouldn't they? But my people have a punishment more fitting than death for such as yourself."

"See how sharp my knife is," John Walking Bear whispered. The moon reflected off the polished steel. "You see Sheriff Carl Brown there is only one way for you to be punished." As the two young men held Carl to the ground he writhed and tried to kick but was helpless in their tight grasps.

Under the light of the bright moon John Walking Bear suddenly reached down. With his left hand he squeezed Carl's testicles and with his right he rapidly sliced the knife, severing the shriveled sac between Carl's legs.

With a scream Carl tried to lurch to his feet, realizing for the first time what had happened. As he threw his head back, his scream piercing the night, John Walking Bear leaned forward. With two fingers he shoved the bloody flesh into Carl's mouth. Then as he nodded, the two younger men released Carl, who lay gagging in the night.

"Perhaps you will be able to drive back to town, Sheriff, or perhaps not. We think that whatever happens now, that your punishment is just." With that the three men left the woods, carefully following the same patches of wet grass among the snow which had brought them tracklessly into the grove.

They left Carl whimpering and retching violently on the ground. He dragged himself back into his car. The bloody path followed him up onto the seat as he sought to leave the woods and save his life.

Carl's sanity was nearly gone now as the Ford lurched back out of the woods. The jumble of trousers and underwear around his legs made maneuvering the pedals almost impossible. Carl whimpered as he spun the car onto the highway. Then, with the accelerator to the floor he began the drive to Montevideo and the only chance to save his life.

"My God, I have to go back," he thought. "I've left my balls on the ground!"

"No, you fool; Go! Keep driving! Just hope you don't bleed to death!"

"But what good am I without my balls?" He questioned himself. And he responded as quickly, "What good are you if you bleed to death over some fucking Indian?"

"Ha, ha!" he chuckled insanely. "That's funny! Bleed to death over a fucking Indian! Ha! Ha! Ha!" Down the highway he raced.

No one will ever know if he might have made the trip to the Montevideo hospital before he bled to death. As he sped along the country road, his mind disoriented, alternately giggling and crying, Carl did not see the patch of ice on the curve ahead of him. He was driving much too fast for the condition of the winter road and when the little Ford began its slide on the ice, Carl realized too late what was happening.

The car lurched violently left and right as it began to leave the road. Bouncing over the snow banked shoulder of the road it almost cleared the ditch completely on the far side. Then it smashed into a stand of small poplar trees where it careened onto its side and slid to a steaming stop deep inside the trees' shelter.

It was shortly after eight a.m. on Monday when a farm family on their way to town spotted the Ford's skid marks and the car back in the trees. Cautioning his family to stay in the car, the man walked through the ditch and into the trees. As he neared the car he recognized the Chippewa County Sheriff's dark Ford, now all bent and mangled in the trees. One look through the window and he knew the man inside was dead, so he looked no further.

The family drove into town and reported what they had found. Only later, when the deputies and ambulance crew were removing Carl's body, did it become known that he didn't carry all of his parts with him to his death.

Chapter
Thirty-seven

"As long as the true cause of the sheriff's death remains a secret, and there's no reason to doubt that it will, people will be satisfied with the newspaper story." Tom began moving toward the depot platform. "I think everyone will be better off believing Sheriff Brown died in an automobile accident when he missed a curve between here and Wegdahl. It's hard to believe so much violence could take place way out here, isn't it? On the surface this appears to be such a peaceful town, but I guess even in the Garden of Eden there was some evil lurking in the shadows."

The heavy rain which had fallen off and on throughout the day had finally turned to snow as they stood talking. The evening sky was filled with huge fluffy flakes. Although the snow melted as fast as it hit the wet ground, it soon would envelop the little prairie town again, even if for only a brief time.

The eastbound passenger train had also entered the station while they said their goodbyes, and now it stood blocking the adjoining street. For a few minutes passengers left or boarded its shining steel compartments. Steam occasionally vented from the safety valves and couplings, and down the track the engineer began the series of movements which would start the train once more on its journey.

Tom moved toward the step and the conductor waited patiently while Tom and Warren said their goodbyes. Pausing for a moment Tom shook Warren's hand. When he turned to Jeanne he thought again of her innocent beauty. Wishing somehow the circumstances had been different, he hugged her gently and with a sad smile he turned toward home.

About the Author

Arthur Norby was raised in rural Minnesota, where he returned to retire in 2010. During the preceding thirty-five years his career as a sculptor took him to many parts of the United States, with twelve years spent in Scottsdale, Arizona.

Over the course of his career he created over a dozen public and monumental sculptures as well as hundreds of decorative sculptures and paintings. All this time the intimate stories of life in rural America told by his father and grandfather occupied his thoughts and led to THE DEADLY WINTER. This is a tale of prejudice and death set in a brutal Minnesota winter and is told in the tradition of those who for generations have passed on their oral history to their families as they enjoyed quiet winter nights.

Also by Arthur Norby, JOURNEY, THE ART OF ARTHUR NORBY, published in 2002 by International Graphics.

Made in the USA
Monee, IL
30 May 2023